CALI MANN

# Peppermint

*Silver Skates, Book 10*

# Contents

# 1

## Pepper

My head nodding along to the Viking metal blasting in my headphones, I sorted the mail into boxes based on address. A letter, letter, porno magazine—I mean, did real tits come that big—bill, bill, magazine—oh, he was hot! I opened the pages to stare at a man's naked chest. With a horned Viking helmet on his head, the muscular man was running down the sandy beach, his dark eyes full of promise. I could certainly use a well-hung Viking about now. The things I could do with his . . . I flipped down the page, but the lower half of his body was regrettably covered by a cloth. *Humph. No love for the single girl.*

Mr. Mulligan made a grumbly noise, slamming his stapler against his desk, and I reluctantly put the magazine in the post box. The lucky customer was getting that delivered, and I was stuck with old and grouchy. Typical. I flipped through a few more letters, then lifted up an off-white envelope covered with Nordic runes. My hand froze. I stared at the envelope. This wasn't one of *those* letters that I often got, the ones to the dead, full of regrets and lost love. But it was strange, just the same.

My boss leaned back in his chair, and it gave a long squeak. My eyes darted to him, and back to the letter. He wouldn't be happy it returned.

I must have put this particular letter in every box in Silver Springs by now, but as soon as I placed it, the addressee changed again, and the customer would return it. I'm sure that wasn't helping my image with my boss any, either. My eyes darted to his balding head bent over his desk, and I gaped at the view behind him. Mr. Mulligan had camped out near the only real window in the place—never mind that I'm the bird shifter and I might want the fresh air, though my boss didn't know that—*and* the tree across the street was on fire. Like really on fire. All burning bush and stuff. Sirens filled the air, and I saw the flash of light off the red fire truck rolling up. I frowned.

My boss, of course, didn't even notice. Just another day in Silver Springs. He slammed his stapler into a stack of papers, then snarled. Picking up the papers, he wrenched them apart and shoved them in the trash can. Then he pecked at his keyboard again, reprinting his mistake.

I bit my lip. I really wanted to run over and see if any hot firemen got off that truck, but I didn't dare. Mr. Mulligan had been yelling at me over every little thing. Whose mail got delivered on time and whose didn't, whose plastic-wrapped magazines disappeared mysteriously into the bathroom with me and returned opened—hey, a girl's got needs—and why I couldn't just turn off that infernal music and listen to him. I shrugged. Not like he could hear it anyway when I used my headphones.

"What is that racket out there?" Mr. Mulligan muttered but didn't look up.

"There's a fire," I said.

2

"Well, that's no excuse to quit working." He grabbed the stack of papers off the printer again and lifted his stapler.

I sighed. Turning the envelope over in my hands, I looked for a clue as to whom it might really belong to, but there was nothing. Just a few scattered runes that when I looked them up online hadn't meant anything to me, and a clearly printed address for Calluna Hernandez. Even as I put it in her box, I knew by the end of the day it'd be back in my hands somehow. It was so frustrating. Mail was meant to be delivered not to keep being returned to the Post Office. At least Mr. Mulligan and I agreed on that point.

I slid the letter into Calluna's box and picked up the next one in my tray. Still, I wondered who had sent the runic letter. They'd been waiting a long time for a response. The envelope didn't seem too much the worse for wear, despite how many boxes it had been through. I must have put it in over a hundred already.

"Pepper!" my boss hollered. He was loud enough that I heard him through the music.

I groaned. I'd known as soon as I saw him pick up the phone that I was in for it again. Reluctantly, I made my way over to him, sliding my headphones down my neck. Feeling defiant, I didn't turn down the volume on the music.

"Mrs. Hart's mail was late again," he growled, standing and coming around his desk to glare at me.

What I expected. I picked up the routes when the carriers were out, and of course, I'd done Donnie's last week. I'd done my best to be punctual, but when the letter addressed to the late Ellen Weston had shown up in my bag, I hadn't been able to ignore it. My cardinal side had taken over, and I'd flown directly to the underworld to deliver it.

Ellen Weston had appeared as an old woman with graying

3

hair. She dropped her knitting at my appearance and jumped up from her rocking chair. "Who are you?"

I grinned. "I'm the mail carrier, and I have a letter for you."

"A letter here?" she'd asked, adjusting her glasses.

"Yes, madam," I said, handing her the envelope. I assumed after death you could be whatever you wanted to be—young, old, hot, boring—but so many of the souls I visited clung to their last human form like they didn't want to forget the life they'd left behind.

Ellen had ripped it open, and her eyes devoured the words on the page. "It's from my grandbabies," she said. "William, Olivia, and Harry."

I grinned wider. I did so love how happy these messages made people.

"I didn't think they'd remember me," Ellen said with tears rolling down her cheeks.

I'd given her a hug and flown straight back to earth, but apparently that hadn't been quick enough for cranky Mrs. Hart.

"Are you listening to me?" Mr. Mulligan yelled, and I nodded.

Most of his head was bald, but tufts of white hair ran along his ears. Behind him, the wall was post office box after post office box, and all I could think was I'd rather be sorting endless piles of mail than listening to his tirade.

"Yes, sir," I replied, hating the squeak in my voice. Was I bird or mouse? I pushed a bit more force into my tone. "It won't happen again."

He went on about how Mrs. Hart was a very important customer, at top volume.

It's amazing how small I feel, even as a grown woman, when someone yells at me. I wanted to pull my headphones back up over my ears, but I forced myself to wait, rather less than patiently. In my mind, I turned Mr. Mulligan's voice into the teacher from Charlie Brown—wah wah wah—but it didn't help much. I tried peering around him, looking for a hot fireman to fantasize about, but I couldn't see any. Oh, there was one! Tall, broad and built for . . . mmm.

"It better not happen again," Mr. Mulligan muttered fiercely.

"Sure thing," I said, eyeing the fireman's ass as he bent over. Even in the bulky uniform, I could make out the shape of his ass and . . . um . . . hose. He could spray me down any time he liked.

My boss scowled at me and shuffled back around his desk.

I took a breath as I watched him go. His back was bent, and wrinkles lined his face. Why hadn't he long since retired? I was sure they'd give him an excellent pension. I grimaced at the path of my thoughts. Mr. Mulligan retiring might be worse for me, the little knot in my stomach reminded me. If they brought in someone younger and more sharp-eyed, he or she might catch me shifting. And if there's one thing I knew about Silver Springs, exposing the magic world to humans was the real no-no.

After readjusting my headphones on my ears, I grabbed a new stack of mail off the cart and headed for the boxes that lined the far wall. Sorting them and placing each letter in the right box was one of my special joys. I always imagined the look on the person's face when they received it, and my heart warmed. I loved mail, and I really did want to be good at my job.

But I couldn't help those other letters either. They found their way into my stack, and I had to deliver them, even if it meant a trip to the underworld, or Mrs. Hart's mail being late. I chewed on my lip. I needed to do better, or Mr. Mulligan was going to fire me. If I was going to keep my job, I needed to start ignoring those letters. The ones addressed to the dead. That's one of the

5

secrets of being a cardinal shifter. A shifter that turns into a bird—not very exciting, right? But the North American cardinal is also a messenger to the afterlife, and people write to their loved ones who have passed. Each letter that crosses my path pulls on my heart strings a little more, and my nature won't let me ignore them. But I was going to have to learn to.

After finishing the pile, I grabbed my coat. "Off on delivery," I said. Donnie was out again today, so I needed to cover his shift.

Glaring at me over his glasses, Mr. Mulligan muttered, "Be punctual. The mail needs to be on time, young lady."

I nodded and waved ducking out the door. *Definitely. No side trips this time.* The mail bag was a comfortable weight on my shoulder. Unfortunately, the firemen and their hoses were long gone. The streets were quiet this afternoon; most people were at work. I'd come to Silver Springs only a short while ago, but it was already starting to feel like home. Small enough that everyone knew your name, but I hadn't grown up here so I wasn't my mother's daughter—Sadie Adar's daughter—you know, the one who got pregnant in high school! Disgraceful!

Moving to Silver Springs had been the best thing I'd done in my life. A fresh start, not haunted by my mother's mistakes. I frowned. Which reminded me that I needed to call her tonight. I'd tried to talk her into moving with me, but she'd insisted she was happy where she was. I couldn't imagine how, but she'd sighed and offered me a peppermint candy. Yes, she'd named me after her favorite treat. "What can I say? I was sixteen," is what she said whenever I complained about my name.

Mom had started working at the library part-time during high school, and afterward the librarian had taken her on as a full-time assistant. Now she was taking classes at the local community college so that she might run her own bookstore someday. I was proud of her. She was reinventing her life at thirty-eight, and she deserved it. Now only if I could make something of mine. I had a good job and I loved the mail, but I had to admit I was lonely. I'd never had many close friends, and I only knew a few people in town. They'd all been nice, of course, even grumpy Mrs. Hart, but . . . I shook my head. That was the problem with a solitary job like this—too much time to think.

My phone buzzed, and I pulled it out of my pocket. Kari's name ran across the screen, and I grinned.

"Have you tried the skates yet?" she asked, breathless.

"Is Hades kissing you again?" I replied snarkily.

She laughed.

"I haven't seen you since you went and got mated," I said, cradling the phone between my ear and my shoulder and shoving the envelopes into the mailbox.

"It's fun. You should try it."

"And doesn't Hades have a job to do somewhere, like say the underworld?" Now I was sounding like a worse grouch than Mrs. Hart. It wasn't fair to treat my friend like this. "I'm sorry, Kari. It's been a rough day."

"It's okay," she said. "What's going on?"

"The usual," I groused. "Mr. Mulligan yelling at me about not being on time."

"You ought to stand up to him," Kari said.

"He's not wrong."

"Yeah, but he doesn't have to be a jerk about it," Kari said. "Why do you have to take the letter right then? Why not wait until after work?"

"Because I have to," I said, shrugging even though she couldn't see me. "There's some kind of urgency to the magic."

7

"Yeah," she said. "It's hard to go against our nature."

I grimaced. "And it's going to get me fired."

"That sucks."

"Yeah, I'm hoping I can control it. I mean, if I really put my mind to it."

"I gotta go, Pep." Kari chuckled at someone else. "I'm sorry. But we'll get together early next week. Maybe Triple E?"

"Sounds good." I was glad Kari was happy, and I couldn't begrudge her hot-as-hell mates.

"And do try the skates," she said.

"But I don't even know how to skate!" I said, but the call had already ended. I laughed. Kari had a way of dragging me into all sorts of things. I didn't know what her obsession with the skates was all about, but it wasn't like I was doing anything else tonight and I'd had a rotten day. I was dying to have some of Candela's special cupcakes anyway—they were better than sex. Or they would be if I'd had any recently. It'd be nice if I could have my own hunky highlander like Kari's mate Callum—or in my case Viking—to sweep me away. I snorted.

* * *

The rink was busy when I arrived. I could see the castle on the hill above, and the ice was surrounded by shops and restaurants. Snowflakes fell lightly here, no matter what the real temperature was. In town, the snow was melting as we moved into spring, but the supernaturals had given the locals some reason why the ice at the rink didn't go with it. It sounded like a bunch of technobabble to me, but whatever, it worked for them.

I'd traded my postal worker uniform for a cozy knit sweater

and jeans. I fingered the soft red cotton and smiled. I'd always been partial to red. Mother said we couldn't help it, it was part of our cardinal nature. Made me wonder if I was going to be looking for a mate with good plumage. I wasn't really into the dandy type. I much preferred someone hunky, muscled, and a little savage. I licked my lips. Probably going to get some use out of Silver Bullet, the silver dildo Kari had bought me at some place called the Magical Rooster, dreaming about hot Vikings and sexy firemen.

Head down, I didn't even notice I'd walked into someone's path. Our bodies collided, and I fell on my ass. Par for the course for me.

"Sorry," I said when I caught my breath, and looked up into fierce green eyes.

"Well, you ought to be," he muttered, pulling his dark coat up closer to his ears, and walked away.

*Thanks for nothing.* I stared after him and grimaced. I dusted myself off as I climbed to my feet. What did I expect him to do? Help me up? Chivalry had died a long time ago. I chuckled. Probably before I was born.

With a mournful look at the cupcake shop, I crossed to the skate rental and waited in line. A mother and her child stood in front of me, the child talking excitedly about the fun to come. Her hands were in red mittens and a red and white pompon sat on top of her hat. She looked like I had at that age but my mother never had time to take me skating, even if I'd had any talent. Mom'd always teased me that I was the clumsiest bird to ever leave a nest, so skating or dance lessons wouldn't have been worth it.

"That's enough, Pepper," I muttered. "Stop feeling sorry for yourself."

When my turn came, I asked for the rental skates Kari had recommended. I stared at the splash of neon green on the side and wondered why I'd even gotten them. I hadn't been kidding when I'd said I didn't know how to skate. But they were mine for the evening, so I might as well try and then go get hot cocoa and cupcakes like I'd intended.

I sat down on a bench, feeling the cold slats through my jeans. After taking off my red sneakers, I put them in my backpack and slid on the skates. They fit me perfectly, even though I was sure Kari and I wore different size shoes. The left shoelace was ripped, but I threaded it through and it seemed to be stable enough. At least if I was going to break a leg, there were plenty of people around to call for help. I'd heard the rink even kept a medic on staff. Which was a good thing with me around. I'd long ago given up being embarrassed about falling on my ass since I did it so often.

Standing, I put my backpack on and clomped my way over to the ice.

"Hey," the attendant hollered. "No bags on the ice."

I frowned and carried mine back to him.

He grinned at me wolfishly. "You're supposed to leave your shoes."

"They're in the bag," I said.

"So you want to rent a locker?" he asked.

"I guess," I said, handing him the card again. I took my shoes out and put the rest of my bag in a locker, before turning to face the ice again. I really didn't think I was going to be here long. This was a disaster in the making.

I'd watched a video online, and the guy made it look so easy. Just push off with one foot and glide on the other. My eyes lit on the little girl with her red hat, doing it so easily, and a rumble of jealousy filled my stomach. I shoved it down. Stupid, being jealous of a kid.

"Hey, Pepper," Neve said as she skated up to me. "You need some help?"

I bit my lip. Her form was perfect.

Neve laughed. "It's not so bad. Honest."

Nodding my head, I reached out a hand, and Neve grasped it, pulling me onto the ice. I glided along from the sheer momentum.

"See!" Neve exclaimed. "Now just push off and glide."

"I know," I said, pushing one leg and letting myself skate. My legs wobbled, and I'd rather be flying, but I could do this. I forced a smile at Neve and said, "Thanks."

"No problem," Neve said, waving as she skated away.

I kept moving along the edge, away from the faster skaters in the middle, but as I moved a strange feeling uncurled in the pit of my stomach. I could feel my mates. There were three, and they were a long way from here. I could feel their rough masculinity through the bond, and they were similar to each other but different. I tried to focus on it and keep my concentration on skating, but I was freaking out.

*How could I have mates?* I couldn't imagine having one mate, let alone multiple. I'd just barely got my life together. I hadn't even dated much, at first terrified of ending up pregnant in high school like mom, but then, just hadn't had the opportunity. What would I do with mates? What would Silver Bullet do? I shook my head, nearly upsetting my center of gravity and waving my arms wildly but caught myself.

My right foot started sliding and there wasn't anything I could do about it. It was like it was happening to someone else. I snorted. I'd always wanted to be a cheerleader —and had always

11

been too clumsy—but this split was going to hurt way more than I ever imagined. Pain ripped up my thighs and I couldn't help the yelp that escaped my lips. As I fell, my cheeks reddened. I kept my eyes down and undid the skates. My breath came in small little pants, and my cheeks were cold with tears. What was I? Bird or mouse? I swallowed then I slowly, painfully, climbed to my feet and returned to the bench.

I looked around, half expecting the guy I'd run into before to be laughing at me— 'cause that was just my luck—but he was gone. At least *he* wasn't my mate. I could still feel the cord pulling on me—to find my mate, to find them, right away. I grimaced and glared at the rink. Why had we linked then? Was there some spell happening here, other than the never-melt one? I frowned and fingered the broken lace on the skates. My gaze narrowed. *Kari!*

# 2

# Skarde

I pressed the ash-covered stick against the parchment, marking out symbols. Four more runes and the message would be finished. In the time we'd been trapped in the underworld, the magic had given us anything we wanted—food, water, fire, weapons. I sure hoped it would give us this—a chance to send a message back to the world.

We hadn't been cursed to a thousand years of torture, just boredom, which for Vikings like us was a fate worse than death. We'd had no visitors; not even Loki's daughter Hel had come to taunt us. I almost believed we'd been forgotten. We'd started marking the days on the wall, but we'd lost count long ago. There was nothing in these bare walls of rock to tell us time was passing. It was a wonder we hadn't gone mad.

We'd been alone, just the three of us, ever since Loki had said the words. He'd wanted his weapon back, the charm I wore around my neck. On the front was the raven's eye of Odin, and on the back, the gem where Loki had hidden enormous amounts of power. Power I couldn't access to rescue us. Power I hadn't been able to resist.

For it was my fault we were here. Being a small chieftain, a magic-user in our village hadn't been enough for me. When a passing minstrel had mentioned how alike my friend Birger looked to Thor, we hadn't paid it much mind. But when the chance had come, to take a gem that Loki imbued with power for his daughter Hel, we'd used that likeness to steal it away. Sheer hubris on my part and I'd condemned my friends, my brothers-at-arms, to the same fate.

Then, in the ultimate trick, I hadn't even been able to access the magic. I wore the icon around my neck and smelled like rot and garbage as a result but could do nothing with it. It might as well have been a bauble I'd stolen in a raid. *Worthless.* I didn't dare take it off, though. It was the only thing we had to trade for our freedom if we ever had the chance.

Over the years, I'd begged Loki to return, to take it back and set my brothers free, but not once had he answered my prayers. The halls we lived in were silent except for our own voices. In the world of the dead and we weren't even haunted. We wandered around and around and never saw anything but clay and rocks. The barren, red clay was burned into our vision until we thought we'd never see anything else again.

We never aged never changed. My own magic stayed exactly as it had been, a few small parlor tricks. We'd tried getting rid of the amulet—burning it, smashing it—but like us, it was unchanging. The same songs, the same stories, the same four walls for what felt like an eternity.

I turned the parchment over in my hands, whispering the magic words that would allow it to reveal its message to who-ever, whatever, now lived in the world above. Then I held it over the flame and watched it burn.

"Please," I whispered, under my breath. My brothers-at-arms slept around me. "Save us."

# 3

# Pepper

Once I'd caught my breath, I stood and inched my painful way toward Candela's Cupcake Shop. I wasn't giving up the treat I'd promised myself for even coming skating, no matter what my injury. My eyes landed on a sign for a skate school. Maybe I should have signed up for classes before going at it on my own. A grimace twisted my lips.

But I had learned something, other than that I was hopeless at anything physical. I'd learned I had not just one mate, but three. I'd seen other shifters around town with more than one mate, but I'd never expected that to be me. In all these years, my mother had never found hers and I thought I'd be the same.

Thora, a tall woman with a white streak in her hair, stood outside Bitchen' Baubles. She winced in sympathy when I passed, and I gave her a half-smile. Candela's cupcakes will make it all better, I promised myself as I limped forward. Hadn't I always said they were better than sex?

The outside of the shops all looked like old-timey cabins with candle lamps. So pretty, like a winter wonderland! Why hadn't I come here more often? I'd spent most of the winter inside the post office, and now that the first flowers were peeking through the snow, here I was at the ice rink.

I stumbled up to Candela's door. In the window was a Christmas candle display with a flickering flame. It was really beautiful. I pretended that I was admiring it and not just leaning against the side of the building waiting for the pain to subside. I should probably have shifted and let it heal, but I was desperate for my treat and I'd limped all the way here.

I stepped inside and headed for the counter. Candela took my order for hot cocoa and a salted caramel cupcake. Her husky cocked his head at me as if he knew about my pain and wanted to help. I forced a smile. Shifters were good like that—we looked out for one another. I glanced over at Candela, wondering if she knew about his shifter nature. She was a human, after all.

When she'd brought my food, I reached into my pocket to pull out the bills I'd stuffed there and pulled out a letter. Not just any envelope, but one covered in Nordic writing and addressed to Peppermint Adar. I gasped. It had never been addressed to me, and I'd never seen it appear before. It'd always been just in the stack of letters. As I stared at the runes, visons of naked well-endowed Vikings danced through my mind. Runes must mean Vikings, right? Weren't they from about that time?

Shaking my head, I paid and thanked Candela, then headed for one of the pink chairs by the wall. Dropping down onto it, I arranged my dishes and stared at the envelope. I considered opening it. It didn't change; the name didn't flicker. Maybe it was actually for me. I blinked. But why hadn't it said so when I'd first seen it?

I slid my finger along the seal and turned it over. Nothing changed. I pushed my nail under the flap. and pulled it open. Then I turned it over just to be sure, and it still read Peppermint

Adar. I opened the envelope and pulled out the paper inside. As I unfolded it, the writing turned from hand scratched runes to clear English. I read it.

"We are trapped. We still live. Loki cursed us to the underworld, to live forever here instead of ascending to Valhalla as was our right. Save us."

I dropped the paper to the table. Then I picked it up again, but the words stayed the same. Valhalla? Loki? Hel? *Vikings had written me a letter?* It must be some kind of joke. I turned the paper over and over but nothing changed. This must be for someone else: a witch, a god—hell, even Hades. They could actually do something about it. I was just a cardinal shifter—a messenger. Who was I to go off rescuing someone?

Besides, hadn't I just said I was going to try to be more reliable? I was going to keep my head down and my eyes on my work. I took a sip of my cocoa. *Dammit.* Mr. Mulligan was going to roast me alive.

But it couldn't hurt to go and see for myself, could it? If they really were Vikings and they were in trouble, someone needed to help them. My fantasies ran through my mind again. Big, buff men with long hair and tattoos and dicks that hung . . . I mean, it wasn't like I was on duty now. I'd planned to shift and heal my wrenched muscles anyway. My shift at the post office didn't start until ten tomorrow. I could just finish my cupcake and do a little run to the underworld to find out what was going on. Maybe the Vikings were fine, they just wanted a little company, and as I hadn't had a whole lot of company myself . . . I was getting as bad as Kari before she met her mates.

*Mates.* These couldn't be them, could they? I took a gulp of my cooling cocoa and considered. More curious than a cat, my mother always said. She'd always pronounced 'cat' like a swear

18

word, which it kind of was to us birds. Another reason I didn't like to deliver Mrs. Hart's mail was the giant yellow house cat who sat in her window and eyed me all the way to the mailbox and back. Intellectually, I knew I was bigger and scarier than him—at least in my human form—but the bird in me quaked.

But even Mom would never have guessed I'd be stalking living Vikings in the underworld tonight. Guess Mom and my's phone chat was going to have to wait. I grinned.

* * *

Darting through the underworld, it hadn't taken me long to find them. Made me wonder why I'd never stumbled on them before, but I could feel the tug of the mate bond in the center of my chest and I had an idea. Still, I pushed it away. There was no way I could be mated to actual Vikings. There must be something about them that would lead me to my true mate. Of course, if they looked like the ones in that TV show . . . if I hadn't been in bird form, I might have wiped the drool off my chin.

The caverns were darker and quieter here, where even the dead rarely traveled. I wondered if I should have approached Hades before I'd come and asked about them. Instead, here I was rushing off again. I sighed, but in my bird voice it came out more of a trill, and the sound echoed against the rock walls.

I veered around a corner and saw the plume of smoke from a small fire and two broad men bent over it. I perched on a nearby rock listening to them talk, and I studied them. They were both good-sized men covered in scraps of leather and furs that despite their bulkiness left little to the imagination. Their skin was tanned as if they'd spent time in the sun, though their letter said they'd been trapped here for a long time. In their hands were curved horns filled with what looked like beer. I took a whiff and smelled the yeastiness mixed with the smokiness of the fire. Birds have a surprisingly good sense of smell. Most people don't think about that, assuming we rely on hearing and sight more.

The fire roared between them, and they spoke gruffly of ancient battles won and lost. One had shoulder-length reddish-brown hair and dark eyes. Around his shoulders, a fur-edged cloak was draped, black on black, and hanging from his neck was a chain with a silver eye on it. A strong beard covered his chin, and his brown eyes glinted with gold in the firelight. If I'd been in human form I'd have been drooling. He was hot.

The other was sandy blond, his hair long and braided across the top of his head and falling down his back. His sapphire blue eyes were striking, and tattoos ran down both sides of his neck. I wanted to reach out and stroke my hand down those marks and see how far they went into the leathers and furs that covered his body.

"To Loki," said the one with the neck tattoos, raising his horn.

"Now, Roar," said the reddish-haired one, digging his stick into the fire. "Don't bring an even worse curse on our heads."

Roar drained his horn. "Do you really think he cares, Skarde? After all this time?"

They seemed like they were from an ancient culture, but I understood them perfectly as if they spoke modern English. *Dead re-enactors?* I chuckled mentally. But the letter said they were real Vikings, alive and trapped. My gaze ran over the rough cave walls, but I saw nothing that would hold them. Then again, magic wasn't always visible even to shifters like me. I grimaced. And we were in the underworld, where there was magic, enough to make Vikings sound like Americans and trap them here for centuries.

'Cursed by Loki,' the letter had said. Well, Loki was real enough. I'd heard Kari talk about him, though I'd never met him. Did that mean they really were Vikings? Ancient and scarred from battle? Neither of them looked that old. I leaned closer, tucking my wings close to my body.

I was so engrossed in trying to figure out the Vikings that I didn't hear a third man approach behind me. He dropped a pouch over me that smelled like old leather, and something tightened over my shoulders, shutting out the light.

"Look, brothers," he exclaimed, striding forward. "I've caught a bird."

The three men had clustered around when my jailor opened the bag. He placed his hand over the top so they could see me between his fingers but there was no place for me to squeeze out. Still, I pecked at him and tried my best.

"A bird?" Roar said, leaning in, his blue eyes bright. "How did it get down here?"

"It's alive," said Skarde, scratching his skin under his heavy fur. His silver eye necklace swung low over me, so close I could have caught it if I had fingers.

"There must be a way to the surface," Roar said. "Do you think it's come to lead us home?"

My gaze jumped between them, but I froze when I glimpsed the one who'd captured me. He was Thor, just as the comics and the movies had imagined him. Flaxen blond hair, muscled chest, and an easy smile. I blinked rapidly, trying to dispel my hallucination—because that's what this had to be, right? Had he knocked me on the head when he'd captured me? I didn't think so—he'd been surprisingly gentle—but how did Thor get here? And he'd been trapped for so many years?

I shook myself. I was being silly. Of course, I knew a couple of gods, including my friend Kari's mate Hades, but it didn't mean that the real Thor looked anything like the visual images we had of him. And there's no way he would have been trapped for one thousand years by Loki. He was too powerful to ever let that happen.

"Well, Birger, let it go," Roar said. "We'll follow it out."

Thor—or rather Birger—grunted.

"Seems unlikely there'd be a crack in the curse," said Skarde, his dark eyes flashing. "After all this time."

There was something off about his scent, even through the sweaty man smell of the others. I didn't expect baths were really a priority down here, but this was something worse than sweat and dirt.

Roar shrugged. "It's worth a try. At this point, anything is. We might even go to Hel again—"

Skarde glared at him, and he went silent.

But Birger frowned and slid his hand aside.

I eyed them all warily. They wanted to leave. I knew that. Why shouldn't I lead them out? They were my mates—wasn't that why I'd come here?

Birger slid the bag down around me to the rock, and I stretched my wings.

They all watched, their eyes full of curiosity.

Taking off, I flew across the cavern. The three men stumbled after me, clumsy on their big feet. I wanted to laugh, but I was going to save them. That made a flutter of warmth rise in my chest. No one deserved to be trapped for this long on the whim of a god. They deserved to be free. I dove through the doorway and spun to see if they followed.

The three Vikings slammed into an invisible wall that showed as black and blue illuminated cracks for mere seconds before disappearing again. Then they fell back in slow motion, yelling out their annoyance. I darted back through the barrier, but I didn't even feel a tickle of magic. There was nothing there for me, but for them, it was a full-on obstacle.

A hand closed around me, and I squawked. It was a very un-cardinal-like sound, more like a chicken. I peered around the bulky fingers and into the dark eyes of the red-head, Skarde. The strange scent of him was stronger, now that I was closer. He smelled like the deep, swampy part of the marsh, sour from standing water. My beak twitched. It wasn't a pleasant smell for someone so sexy, and I couldn't help being a little disappointed. He tilted his head and stared at me, his dark eyes swirling as if they saw behind my bird form. Did he know what I was?

Then suddenly, I did feel some kind of magic sliding over me, smooth like silk but with a cold, slimy feel. I twitched. A cage formed around me, squeezing me even more than the fingers had until I thought my heart would explode. Instead, my human form burst out from the bird and I fell naked to the floor. The warriors gathered around me, and I stared up at them blinking.

"What the hell?" I gasped. I'd never been forced from my shifter form before. I'd never come out naked either; usually my clothes reformed with me. I could feel the heat rising in my cheeks, though the rest of me shivered in the cold cavern.

"A woman?" Birger asked, confusion in his voice.

A slow smile spread across Roar's face, and he leaned in closer. "A beautiful woman."

Skarde just watched me, stroking his eye pendant.

"Got a blanket I can borrow?" I asked, trembling harder under his gaze. Though I had to admit the strange warmth that rose in my gut at the obvious interest in their gazes. They took in every inch of me and didn't seem to find me wanting. You'd think such big, virile men would want a warrior woman, not me. Maybe they'd been here too long and any woman was looking good. That thought soured my mood somewhat, and I stood, a bit wobbly, and glared at them. "A blanket?"

They frowned at me.

I sighed. I'd understood them. Surely, they understood me. "I'm cold."

"I'd be happy to warm you up," Roar said, offering me a hand.

Meeting his fierce gaze, I suddenly wasn't cold anymore, but I didn't want them to know that. They might be the sexiest men I'd ever seen, but I had a mission. I crossed my arms over my chest and raised an eyebrow at them. "I'm here to rescue you."

# 4

## Pepper

They laughed, hard, uproariously. Their whole bodies shook with it.

I frowned. Didn't Vikings respect women warriors? Shield-maidens and all that? "What's so funny?"

"It's as you said," Skarde said, trying to wipe away the smile on his face. "The little birdie is here to save us."

Roar laughed even harder, slapping his knee.

And Birger just quaked, amusement in his sparkling blue eyes.

I put my hands on my hips, forgetting my nakedness, and demanded, "Again, why is that so funny?"

Birger arched a blond eyebrow. "You have to admit it's hilarious. A tiny, brown bird like you saving us?"

That was the last straw, mocking my lack of bright red color. Why did the male birds get the best plumage? I spun, turning my back to them. "Fine," I said, marching toward the exit.

A muscled arm wrapped around me, and I was pulled back against fur and skin. I tried to keep myself stiff, but I couldn't help curling into the sheer heat of him. I turned and met Roar's deep, sapphire eyes.

"Not so fast, little one," he said. "We have some questions."

"Good," I said. "So do I."

He grunted, his hand curling around my ass, and I squawked.

Roar winked. "Don't worry, little one, I've never taken a woman who wasn't willing."

Then he led me over to the fire. Wrapping me in furs, he pulled me down next to him on the rock. His bare leg pressed up against me, and even through the thick furs I could feel it. I wanted to pull off his clothes and take him as mine right then. *Mates*, my bird trilled, and I couldn't help my hand running along his side. He grunted, but he didn't stop me.

The others had followed, gathering around us. Their gazes were on me, hot and full of heat. Even humans felt the effects of the mate bond. It just made them really lusty. I glanced up, meeting Birger's eyes as he offered me a horn filled with beer. I swallowed at the sheer passion in them. Hadn't I always dreamed of Thor looking at me that way? Now was my chance. I was already naked.

Shaking my head, I took the horn and drank. *Save the Vikings first, then fuck them.* I repeated it to myself like a chant. I took another long swallow and eyed the men. "How do you live down here? With no water or food?"

"The magic provides for our needs," Skarde said, waving his hand. "Whatever we want appears."

"Except women," Birger said, the sadness in his voice almost comical, but the intensity in his eyes was no joke.

Heat flushed through me, but I forced myself to ask, "Is that how you wrote the letter?"

Skarde tilted his head at me again. His mannerisms were so bird-like, I could almost imagine him as a shifter, but he didn't feel like one. Not that it would be easy to tell anything with

26

the fog of foul magic that surrounded him. "You received our message."

I nodded. "It came through the Post Office."

They frowned at me. "What is this Post Office?"

I blinked. I'd assumed that the same magic that allowed us to understand one another, though we spoke different languages, would explain things, but there must be a limit. "A messenger service."

Skarde leaned forward, taking my hand in his. I should probably have pulled away. I hardly knew them, and they wouldn't know what this mate bond was. He didn't do anything though, just held it and said, "How long has it been? Up there?"

"Since there were Vikings?"

"Our kind is gone?" Skarde asked, his voice hard.

Birger said, "Yes, since there were others like us." He scooted in on my other side so I was sandwiched between him and Roar.

I licked my lips. "One thousand years." I expected surprise; I didn't expect the deep resignation on their faces. I lay my hand on Birger's thigh and pressed my leg against Roar's. Comfort for a shifter involved touch. I wasn't sure if it was their love language too, but they accepted it.

"You got the message and came to save us," Birger said, laying an arm across my shoulders and squeezing. "That was very brave."

I gave him a smile.

"And you came bearing what weapons?" Roar asked, his voice soft against my other ear. I hadn't realized how close he was to me, but I didn't really want him to move away.

"My brains," I said fiercely. It wasn't like they had anyone else, and I was their mate.

Skarde studied me, rubbing his beard. The others started

to laugh again, and he made a motion with his hand. "The Trickster placed us here. It might be worth hearing her ideas."

"We have tried," Birger said, a frown indenting his broad forehead. "Many weapons, many magics, and fire—nothing has worked."

"Vikings are good at brute force," Skarde said, a wry grin on his face.

The other two nodded, their shoulders slumping.

I frowned at him. He was different from the others. He was still broad, muscled, and looked like he'd spent his life in battle. The foul magic surrounded him, but there was something else under there. Was he a witch?

"What should we try?" Birger said.

I blinked, suddenly unable to think of a single idea. Who did I think I was? I had no idea how to save them. I was just a bird shifter. Other than my ability to travel to the underworld, I had no special magic. I certainly couldn't undo a curse that Loki had made, and it wasn't like it seemed to have weakened over the years. I couldn't even see the magic, except for that brief moment when they struck it. They had battered at the barrier over and over again and gotten nowhere. "You've tried running at it and attacking it?"

"Yes," they said.

I tilted my head. "Have you ever tried walking though, maybe backwards? Loki is a trickster after all."

Birger stood up and strolled toward the doorway. I couldn't help admiring his well-shaped ass as he walked away. A shifter always recognized the mate bond, and it had snapped into place as soon as I'd arrived. Not for just one of them, but for all three. I'd been trying to ignore it and my body's almost instant reaction to these three men. I shook my head. *Focus, Pepper, focus. Drool later.*

I chewed on my lip. Birger was moving slower as he approached the barrier, but he had a determined look on his face. I appreciated that they were desperate and willing to try anything at this point. They were brave Vikings and they'd been here for . . . well . . . a really, really long time.

He reached out a hand as he got to the doorway and waved it ahead of him. The blue lines appeared around it as soon as it touched the barrier. He pulled it back and held it against his chest, glancing over at us. Then he turned around and backed into the doorway. The lines radiated around him, and he groaned in pain. But he kept going until he couldn't any longer, the magic holding him like a fly in a web.

"Get out," I called to him.

Birger tried to shift back into the cave, but the magic held him fast. He gave another grunt, pain running over his face.

I stood, immediately moving toward him. I could feel his agony running down our connection. "He's hurt."

Roar and Skarde hurried over, grabbing Birger's arms and yanking him back out of the magic. Burns covered his neck and arms, anywhere that hadn't been covered in his clothes. He sank to the ground, and Skarde waved a hand over his back.

I gasped and reached out to touch his face. "Oh, Birger, I'm so sorry."

He smiled gently. "It was worth a try, little bird."

"The name's Pepper," I said softly. "Peppermint."

"Beautiful." His hand traced along my cheek, and heat swept through me.

I licked my lips. The mate bond urged me to take him, right now, right there. It didn't care that I'd just met him, and neither did he from the passion in his eyes. I leaned in closer and pressed my lips to his. He kissed me back, and I drowned in the sweet, nutty taste of him.

When I came up for air, he grinned and pulled me to him. Everywhere our skin met, my nerves caught fire. I lifted my leg and threw it over him, trying to get closer, needing to touch every part of him. My bird sang within me. This was our mate, one of them, and he was ours to claim.

Birger ran a finger along my lips and said hopefully, "Another?"

I chuckled and kissed him again. It didn't matter that we'd just met. It didn't matter that the others were here. Nothing mattered but the feel of him under me. Our kiss deepened, and I was lost.

My nipples budded in the cool air as my blanket fell away. Birger's hard cock pressed against me through his clothes. I gasped. Heat filled my core, chasing away any chill even though I was still naked. My fingers ran over his chest and down to the ties of his pants, untying them. I slid beneath the fabric and grasped his hardness, stroking it. He moaned, reaching for me.

I shoved down his pants, needing him inside me. As soon as he was free, I lowered my soaking wet self onto him. He reached for my breasts, cupping them and flicking the already hardened nipples. We moved together as if we'd always done this, and I gasped at the intensity of the sensations coursing through me. I closed my eyes, focusing on the rhythm, taking him to the cliffs with me. I came throwing back my head and crying out, and he did too.

Afterward, I stood and glanced up at our admiring audience. In our passion, I'd completely forgotten they were there. I'd forgotten they were human and I was going to take the mate bond slow for them. They wouldn't know what this was. They'd think I was some crazed, sex-obsessed chick. I blinked. But they'd feel it too, the passion and the lust, wouldn't they?

"Um . . ." I said. I'd come here to help them, not to sleep with them. What they needed right now was a way to escape not a lover. *Crap.* "I'll find a way to get you out."

They just looked at me.

"Okay?" Then I shifted into a bird and took off. I needed help.

\* \* \*

I walked up the steps of Kari's house. The crescent moon was in the sky above, and I knew it was late. Yet, I couldn't help the urgency that rolled under my skin. My mates were in trouble, and I needed to do something. Every shifter bone in my body called out for it. I knocked on the door.

I'd hated leaving the Vikings in the underworld. They'd assured me it made no difference to them. They'd been there forever and a few more days wouldn't hurt. I needed to go in search of a way to help them. The only thing we could come up with was finding Loki. But as I well knew from Kari's adventures, Loki was not someone who could be found if he didn't want to be found. I didn't even know what the trickster god looked like or where he was. The only people I knew who might be able to find Loki were Kari and her mates.

If I wasn't a shifter, this instant connection I felt to all three of them—Skarde, Roar, and Birger—might have been weird. In fact, it was probably strange to them, except maybe Skarde. I didn't really understand this feeling about him. He was supernatural in some way.

No one came to the door, so I knocked again, louder. *Come on.*

The door swung open, and my mouth dropped open. Hades

stood there a towel wrapped around his waist. I might have been mated but I was still a hot-blooded woman. I was totally looking at his long hair and chocolate brown eyes and not the bulge against his tiny white towel.

"Yes?" he asked, his voice as smooth as butter.

I shook myself. I wasn't interested in ogling other people's mates. Mine were in trouble, trapped in the underworld. I blinked at Hades. The underworld. "Hades."

"That is my name," he said, scratching his neck and holding his towel with the other hand.

"Um—" I swallowed. "There's some men . . . um . . . some Vikings trapped in the underworld."

"Yeah?"

"I want to get them out." I felt ridiculous. I was having a fairly normal conversation, but I was acting like a schoolgirl. "Loki cursed them."

Hades shrugged. "Why don't you ask him, then?"

"That's why I came here, to ask Kari how to find Loki, but since they're in your world . . ." I bit my lip.

He rubbed his chin. "More like on Hel's side."

Why didn't I think of that? Of course Loki's daughter, Hel, would be involved. "Could you get them out?"

He frowned. "Free them from Loki's curse? No."

"Oh," I said, nodding. "Do you know where Loki is, so I can ask him?"

He shook his head. "No, but maybe Kari knows." He stepped back, gesturing for me to come in.

"Thank you," I said, moving forward through the doorway and into the living room.

"Who was it?" Kari asked, strolling through the door.

She wore her robe, but she had that after-sex glow that just seemed to follow her around since she'd been mated. I was happy for my friend. She totally deserved the happiness she'd found with Hades, Dagen, and Callum the highlander.

"Pep!" Kari exclaimed. "What's wrong?"

I walked into my friend's arms, and she smelled like vanilla and amber. Bone deep, I felt the tiredness of a full day of work, my skating mishap, and a journey to the underworld.

"I fell on my ass," I said.

"Was it like the time you made Reggie eat your vag?" she asked, a twinkle in her eye.

I could feel the heat washing over my cheeks remembering the scene with Reggie the bouncer at Vee. No one can embarrass you quite like a girlfriend.

"No," I muttered. Then trying to get the focus off me, I glanced sheepishly toward Hades. "Doesn't he ever wear clothes?"

Kari grinned. "No. Isn't it fab?"

I snickered.

"So, what's going on?" she asked, dropping down onto the couch. "Hades, hon, can you bring us the wine?"

"Is this a one bottle of wine kinda night?" He raised an eyebrow. "Or two?"

"We'll see," Kari said with a wink.

Hades chuckled and headed off toward the kitchen.

"Did you know the skates were going to do that?" I sank onto the couch next to her.

"Do what?" she asked with a grin. "Besides, I thought you didn't skate."

"I don't," I growled. "I don't know how I let you talk me into it. I just had such a rotten day."

"Mr. Mulligan on your case again?" Kari winced in sympathy.

I nodded. "So I went, even though I knew I shouldn't, and like usual, I made a fool of myself."

She chuckled and covered her mouth. "Sorry, Pep."

I sighed. I went on to tell her about the mate bond and the Vikings and their predicament.

"I do envy you shifters and that instant knowledge," she said, taking a wine glass from Hades. "Dagen told me about it, and it would have saved so much trouble with everyone else."

"But they're human, well, I think so anyway. They won't know."

"Hum," she said, sipping her drink.

"What should I do?" I asked, taking the other.

"Well, obviously, you have to go to Loki and get him to undo the spell."

I took a gulp of my wine. "Right? But who says he'll help? And maybe he's still mad at them?"

Hades snorted. I'd almost forgotten he was in the room. "He probably doesn't even remember casting the curse."

Kari smiled at him. "Anything you can do? The underworld is your domain."

He ran a hand through his hair. "I can't undo a curse cast by another god."

"Can you get them out? So they can go to Loki and demand forgiveness?" Kari asked.

"Demand?" he asked, looking offended. "He is a god."

Kari looked at him over her wine glass, and I almost snorted my own drink. I was glad I didn't have to deal with the pressure of that. It was enough to be a messenger to the underworld and a shifter.

"You didn't answer the question."

I grinned at my friend. Kari always had the best ideas. Well, other than the dancing on the bar bit. I hadn't meant to go crashing into Reggie, and I didn't know which of us was more embarrassed. Turning to Hades, I asked, "Can you?"

He groaned. "Yes, but it will only be temporary."

"How temporary?"

"One week," he said. "If you can't find Loki in that time, back to the underworld they go."

*Only one week?* My heart sank. How was I supposed to find Loki in so little time?

"Why one week?" Kari asked, tilting her head.

I had to admit, I was burning with curiosity too. It was such a random and completely set period of time. Did Hades know something about the spell that we didn't? Maybe it was possible to undo that soon.

"Why are flames orange?" he asked, shrugging. "Why is the sky blue?"

"Surely you can give them more time," she said skeptically.

"I can't," he said, turning and stomping away.

Kari and I looked at each other. A week wasn't much time.

"Do you think Loki's still around?" I asked.

"I don't know," Kari said. "Why did he curse your Vikings?"

I stared at her. "You know, I didn't even ask. What an idiot I am. What if they were cursed because they were evil?"

Kari shook her head. "No, Pep, you wouldn't be mated to someone evil."

"How do you know?" I looked at my empty wineglass. I hadn't even remembered drinking it.

"Because you're a good person. The Fates wouldn't be so unkind," she said patting my hand.

I pressed my lips together. People didn't get anything in this world for being good people. My mom had been a good person,

35

and she'd ended up pregnant at fifteen. I remembered the foul magic smell around Skarde. Could he have been practicing something evil? I mean, I was sure being trapped for all this time would make you desperate to try almost anything, right? I sighed and took a sip of my now empty glass.

"More?" Kari asked, lifting the bottle.

"When does their time start?" I asked, glancing toward the door.

"Hades won't make it start until tomorrow," she said.

I held up my glass.

* * *

The next morning, I found myself curled up on Kari's couch with a throw tossed over me and an enormous dog snoring next to me. Hade's mastiff was the biggest animal I'd ever seen, and I felt tiny next to it.

"Hey, Box," I said, rolling over. Pain shot through my head. Maybe we had slightly more to drink than we intended. That's usually how it happened with Kari.

My feet touched the floor and something hard and round. I leaned over, holding my head, and peered blearily at the collection of bones by the couch. One of them was a skull. Presents from Hade's pet, I assumed. Where *did* he get those things?

Lifting my head, I realized I was alone in the living room. I sure didn't want to go wandering around and stumble into more of my friend's half-naked mates. I should just go back to my apartment and grab some medicine. Thank goodness I didn't have to work today . . . did I?

I patted around the couch looking for my purse and my phone.

I'd had to go home before coming over here last night since I'd lost my clothes with the Vikings. I was still kind of sad about that red sweater. It was one of my favorites. My hand closed on my phone, and I brought it to my face. I glared at the alarm going off on the screen. Work in ten minutes. *Hell no.* I jerked toward the door and cried out at the pain in my head. Why had I done it? Kari always got me in the worst situations. We'd met getting drunk at a wedding, and it had set the tone for our whole friendship.

I needed to get home and call work or something. I shoved open the front door and tripped on the step, falling into muscled arms. A foul magic smell swept over me and I looked up into a Viking's brown eyes. "Skarde . . ."

He smiled.

". . . how are you here?" I squinted into the bright sunlight and looked at Roar and Birger and behind them, Hades.

Hades at least looked sheepish. "You didn't want them today?"

I forced my lips to curve up despite my hangover. "Of course. They needed to be set free and find Loki . . ."

"Too much drink, little bird," Birger said, laying his hand on my shoulder.

"Skarde." Roar indicated my head.

The Viking holding me lifted his hand and swiped it across my forehead. Sparkles shone in front of my eyes, but the pain was gone. "Magic? Are you a witch?"

"No," Skarde said gruffly, standing me on my feet.

I frowned, studying him. "Is it the word? Does it offend you somehow?"

Roar whistled, looking at the house behind us. "What is this castle?"

37

"It's Kari's house," I said, looking around for Hades, but he had apparently washed his hands of my mess. "But I need to get to work—"

"No worries, little one," Roar said. "We'll just explore." He punched Birger's arm. "Time to find us some women."

A fierce growl escaped my mouth. They were *my* mates. There was no way they could go running off with other women. I scowled at them, and Roar smirked.

Skarde touched my arm. "They can't see the threads."

I spun toward him. "You *are* a witch."

He grimaced. "I have some magic, yes. Enough to see the orange mate threads that run between us."

My mouth dropped open. I'd never heard a witch describe it before. "You know what I am?"

"A beast-man," he said.

I snorted. "We call people like me shifters."

He nodded.

My alarm went off on my phone again, and my eyes jerked to the screen. I was late, and I couldn't leave the Vikings to fend for themselves. I dialed the Post Office.

"Mr. Mulligan," I said, using my best scratchy voice and cough for effect. "Yeah, I don't know what happened. I'm not feeling well."

My boss was terrified of sickness, so this always worked. "Yes, sir, as soon as I'm better." I coughed, then clicked the off button. When I turned back to the Vikings, I found all three gaping at me.

"What is that thing?" Roar asked, pointing at my phone.

# 5

# Roar

"It's a cell phone," she said, distraction in her voice.

I moved closer to look at the odd glow emanating from the box in her hand. It was as bright as a fallen star, especially when the morning sun hit it. I reached my hand up to touch it, and it chirped like a bird.

The woman put it up to her ear and said, "Hi, Mom."

"What's a Mom?" I asked, admiring the shape of our woman, here in the clear sunlight. She was beautiful—tiny, but with curves in all the right places. Her leggings clung to her hips, and it was almost as if she were naked again. My cock rose, begging for a taste, and I grinned.

She frowned at me and turned away. "Yes, I've got to work all day. I can call you later in the week."

I looked back at Birger and Skarde, who shrugged. We understood her words for the most part, although they didn't seem as clear as they'd been in the underworld. But I had a feeling this new world was going to be full of strange and wondrous things. I'd enjoyed her growl when we mentioned finding some women, even if Skarde and Birger laughed at me for calling her ours, but she was. There was some connection there, more than rescuer, more than the first woman we had seen in ages, just more.

Someone stepped out of the house, and I raised my spear. My brothers joined me, weapons in hand. Birger carried his favorite hammer and Skarde an ax, and we were as ready to fight as we'd been one thousand years ago.

The man in strange clothes took in our appearance and pulled out a shiny blade, shouting, "Some fun at last!"

We screamed our battle cry and attacked the strange man. He fought expertly with his sword, attacking and parrying. I growled. We were three against one, so no doubt we'd prevail, but this was fun. Our weapons clanged together, and our woman spun from her conversation with the box, her mouth gaping.

I whooped. For our woman to see us in battle—how proud she'd be at our virility. We circled the man, and he parried our thrusts. The sun beat down on us from above, and the air was brisk and cold. I felt alive in a way I hadn't felt in centuries.

"Mom, gotta go," she said into the shiny box.

My spear jabbed at the man's waist, and he winced.

"Really can't talk right now," she said, then dove into the midst of our fight. Our little bird waved her hands. "Stop, Callum, Vikings! Right now!"

We froze, our weapons in the air, even the new man.

"Aww, lass, it's just a bit of fun," he said.

She spun and shoved her finger into his face. "I don't want to hear it, Callum. You've been here long enough; you know better."

His shoulders slumped, and I couldn't help the snort that escaped me.

Our shield maiden turned back to us. "And you, boys," she

said in perfect disgust. "You are my responsibility, and this world is very different from the one you left. No one fights with weapons like that."

Birger shrugged. "He did have a sword."

She rolled her eyes. "He's an anomaly and you shouldn't follow his terrible"—she glared at Callum—"example."

We hung our heads, thoroughly chastised.

She looked back and forth between us and raised her finger to tap her chin. "If you're going to be in the modern world, you're going to dress like us."

"But you are hardly wearing anything," I said. Not that I minded in her case, but the stranger could certainly use some furs.

"Come on," she said, marching down toward where the grass ended and the hard rock began. She pressed a button, and after a strange chirp, walked around and opened a door on a weird cart. Well, it had wheels like a cart and a top and was bright red. "Get in."

"Get in what?" Skarde asked.

"This is a car," she said.

"A mode of conveyance, like a cart," said the strange man unhelpfully.

"Where are the horses? Or oxen?" I asked.

"They're invisible," she said with a sigh and disappeared within the box.

We all rushed forward, weapons still out, peering at the cart. There wasn't anything that seemed dangerous, and besides, our clan was known for its bravery, so we put the weapons away. I opened the door and slid inside next to our woman, and the others got in the back. There was a small click noise, and I frowned at her.

She grinned. "Just so you can't fall out."
Then she did something magic, and the beast roared to life.

# 6

## Pepper

I pulled up to the thrift store, with my Vikings in tow. When I glanced over at them, I couldn't help snorting. They were all white-faced as sheets. My laughter erupted as I climbed out of the car. They scrambled out after me, spinning and raising their weapons at the vehicle.

"Foul beast!" Birger hollered.

"Angry god," Roar muttered, poking it with his spear.

"Is it alive?" Skarde asked, his eyes nervously darting around.

"No, it's not a living thing," I said, flipping through my wallet and hoping I had enough money. I hadn't expected to be buying clothing for a bunch of Vikings today. I grinned. Not that I really expected that any day.

"How does it go?" he asked, closer to me than he'd been before.

"Magic," I said. I considered explaining machinery to them, but I figured this was an easier reason for the moment. Magic was something they understood.

He rubbed his beard, studying the car. "What strange ways you have, Pepper."

I winked. "You haven't seen anything yet." Turning to the others, I continued, "Put away your weapons. There are no battles here."

They frowned but did as I asked.

I sighed in relief. I'd brought them outside Silver Springs to shop because there was no way I was getting caught by my boss in town when I was supposed to be ill and in bed. "This," I said, gesturing to the storefront, "is where we buy clothes."

The Vikings looked suitably impressed.

"Remember," I admonished. "No weapons!"

They grumbled, but they followed me inside. The sleepy clerk raised an eyebrow at our parade, and I half-whispered, "Viking re-enactors."

She sniffed, and an odd look overcame her face like she'd just smelled the worst silent fart. I took a whiff, but I didn't smell anything.

The clerk's scowl followed us back into the store.

I blinked. Did they smell bad? Living in a cave all this time, I doubt they had access to running water and a shower. Sponge baths could only do so much. But I hadn't smelled anything unpleasant, and I was a shifter—we scented everything. I had been bothered by the foul magic but was there more dirt and grime stuck in their furs?

"What died in here?" a guy asked, walking down the aisle next to us.

*Shit.* They must have the underworld stink still on them. We needed to get what we needed and get out of here quickly before we were thrown out. I pushed them toward the racks of blue jeans and grabbed a variety in different sizes then tossed some shirts on top of them. We went straight to the dressing rooms and I pointed to each one.

"Roar, go in there and take off your clothes. You in there, Skarde, and you in there, Thor . . . I mean Birger." They followed my directions without any argument, and I was on the verge of a sigh of relief . . . when Roar tumbled out of the dressing room with his linen pants around his ankles.

"What trickery is this?" he exclaimed.

I dropped the clothes on a nearby shopping cart and ran over to him. He didn't seem injured, other than his clumsy fall. I frowned. "What happened?"

The others peered around the doors of their dressing rooms like shy old ladies, not wanting to be left out of the excitement.

"Magic," Roar said, gripping my arm.

I looked in his dressing room, and I didn't see anything out of the ordinary—a hook, a bench, and a mirror. "What?"

"Me in the wall! How could I be two places at once?"

I couldn't help the laughter that tumbled out of me. Tears rolled down my cheeks. "You mean the mirror?"

Birger chortled. "You've seen such things before. Remember that village we raided with the pretty"—his eyes went to me—"horses?"

I guessed I'd scared them more than I thought with my outburst earlier. As Skarde had said, they didn't know about the mate bond, and it was normal for them to want women after all this time. Even if it made me seethe. The thought killed my humor, though, and I muttered, "Horses?"

Birger nodded. "Yup, and how they kept those things to help them do their hair."

A jealous knot uncurled in my stomach, and I slapped it down. Those women had lived a thousand years ago, and they'd been raiding their village, so it wasn't like they'd made love with them. I couldn't blame them for what they'd done before they'd met me, their true mate, and they couldn't see the mate bond. Not really. Maybe if I kept telling myself this, I'd come to believe it.

I helped Roar to his feet, ignoring his red cheeks, and sent him back into the dressing room. Then I handed each of them jeans of various sizes over the top of the doors, explaining that they were pants and they should tell me when a pair fit.

"It fits," Birger said, strolling out with his jeans unbuttoned and his enormous dick hanging out.

It seemed that it was my turn to blush red as a strawberry. I glanced side to side for onlookers as I rushed over. Luckily, there didn't seem to be anyone nearby. My hormones exploded, and I wanted to take his length in my hand right there. I remembered all too clearly how it felt pumping within me. I gritted my teeth and explained to him that the penis goes inside the pants.

I held my hands at my sides as he did so. My cheeks burned even hotter, but I kept my eyes averted. Who would have thought that Vikings would be so well-endowed? Well, *I had*, in every fantasy I'd ever imagined. Then I told him to zip and button them, and he frowned at me.

"No ties?"

"No," I said, reaching out and doing up the fastenings for him.

His hands came around mine, and I looked up into his sky-blue eyes. I swallowed as warmth swirled through my nether regions, and I wished we were anywhere but here.

"Let me finish," I said.

"Of course, little bird," he said, his voice deepening. "Pep-per."

Then I handed him a t-shirt. He pulled it on, and it stretched across his muscular chest. My chin dropped to the floor. I didn't really want to tell him it was too tight, but I probably should. He pulled on it as if the material could stretch any more than it already had. The other two came out of their dressing rooms in various states of dress, but they had at least listened to the penis goes in the pants bit. Once I had them in decent fitting pants and shirts and I'd tossed a few extra over my arm, we wrapped their furs up in a big bag and headed to shoes.

Looking at the lines of worn shoes, Skarde lifted his leg. "What's wrong with our boots?"

My gaze followed the line of his muscled calf and thigh, and I choked out, "Nothing, but you've been wearing them for all this time." I picked up some sneakers. "Why not give something else a try?"

He crossed his arms over his chest. "I'm not wearing someone else's dirty shoes."

Who knew that Vikings would be so picky? I'd known they kept their hair well-groomed, but I hadn't known it extended to not wearing used clothing. *I better not tell them about their shirts and pants.* "Okay, let's get the pants and shirts, and we'll go elsewhere for shoes."

They nodded, and we approached the clerk. They leaned over and let her snip the tags off their clothing, and her hand ran along Birger's arm. I snarled like an alley cat, and she backed off.

Birger's mouth twisted as if he was holding back a grin.

Then we headed back out to the car, dropping their old clothes in the back.

A little boy and his mom walked by us, and the kid stage whispered, "Are they wrestlers?"

*Wrestlers?* I guess the long hair and the muscles? I had to admit they were just as hot in t-shirts and jeans as they'd been in leathers and furs. Their leather boots actually looked good with those pants, almost like cowboys—another dirty fantasy of mine.

"Pepper," Skarde said, breaking my spell. "We are hungry."

I grinned. "Of course you are. Shopping always makes one hungry."

They looked at each other, bewildered, and shrugged. When I headed back to my car, they followed along more reluctantly.

"Must we ride in the beast again?" Birger asked.

The others grunted.

"Yes," I said. "You're in the modern world now. You're going to have to get used to some things."

Their faces fell.

I grimaced. Might be enough adventures for their first morning here. "But maybe not all at once. Let's go home, and I'll order pizza."

"What is pizza?" Roar asked as we climbed in the car.

"Meat pie," I said, and a chorus of gleeful shouts met my ears.

* * *

Back at my apartment, the Vikings never seemed to tire of questions. I showed them the kitchen and the fridge. They gazed at my pitiful groceries with wide-eyed wonder.

"It keeps them cold?"

Roar flicked on and off the kitchen light like it was a magic trick. I showed them the bathroom and tried to explain how to use the toilet, and they erupted into peals of laughter like ten-year-olds.

"Why can't we just pee outside?" Roar asked.

"Because my neighbor doesn't like it when people pee on her

azaleas," I said, trying to keep a straight face. Then I continued, "This is a big town with lots of other people, and no one wants to see your dicks."

They smirked at me, and I sighed. I guess jumping Birger in the cave had already made them think I was easy. Not that anything was simple when a mate bond was involved. "Just use the damn toilet."

We just peeked in the bedroom, then hurried onward to the living room. I used the magic excuse as long as I was able because it was simple and something they already understood. Eventually, I'd have to explain to them about technology, but it seemed like a conversation best left for when we knew they really were staying in the modern world. But what if they weren't? I shoved the thought down. We had a week. We had to find Loki.

I set them up in front of the TV and showed them how to work the remote.

"What the hell is that?" Birger growled, jumping back, his hammer in his hands.

Roar had his spear out, and Skarde gripped his amulet. What was it about Vikings that everything required a weapon?

"It shows pictures of people and tells their story," I said. "Like a dream."

Skarde scowled. "Is it a drug?"

"No, it's technology," I said, but they all looked at me oddly. I sighed. "I meant it's magic. It can't hurt you. It's just for entertainment."

"What's entertainment?" Birger asked.

"Fun," I said. "Didn't you have storytellers?"

Skarde nodded. "We'd listen to them around the campfire."

"This is a magic storyteller."

They frowned, but sat down, watching the screen warily. The furniture was worn and used, but under the Vikings, my couch and armchair looked tiny and fragile too. I hoped they wouldn't break them. I flinched when Birger resettled his weight, leaning his hammer against the arm. Skarde pressed the remote buttons and stopped at some historical show. I squinted. *Figures.* Vikings.

"Why are they fighting in an open field?" Roar groused. "It's stupid."

Skarde laughed. "When there are perfectly good bushes to hide behind?"

Birger snorted.

I smiled. That should keep them entertained for a bit while I ordered food. Grabbing my cell phone from my bag, I stepped away and dialed Anthony's Pizza. I ordered three extra-large meat pizzas for delivery, then clicked off the phone.

"What is that device?" Roar said, his arms sliding around me. Just as I had the first time he held me, I couldn't help sinking into his warmth. The mate bond pulled on me and didn't want me to waste another second. Once we mated, shifters went to bed and sometimes didn't come out for days until the first urge was satisfied. It wasn't like any other sex we'd ever had in our lives. It was intense. It was all-consuming.

And I'd gotten not one mate, but three stunning Vikings, a literal fantasy come true. I wanted to wait and give them time to adjust to the modern world, to me, but my body wanted me to claim them now. I chewed on my lip. What if I never got another chance? What if this week was all we had? What if we weren't able to break the spell?

"You didn't answer," Roar said, stroking his finger along my cheek.

I turned in his arms and looked up into his deep blue eyes. If this was all we got, shouldn't we take advantage of every opportunity we had? When he leaned down to kiss me, I didn't resist. His lips were warm and velvety, and I couldn't help the groan that escaped me. When he scooped me up and carried me into the bedroom, it was every fantasy that I'd ever had—come true. I wrapped my arms around his neck, tracing the lines of his tattoos. "What do they mean?" I asked, my voice husky.

"Badges of honor," he said.

He lay me on the bed and peeled my clothes from me, kissing each revealed inch. I trembled under his touch, trying to reach for him again, and he caught my hands above my head, holding fast. He nibbled at my shoulder, at the curve of my neck, and down to my breasts. I vibrated with sensation as my nerves raced to the surface, crying out for his touch, and I wriggled against his hold.

His knee nudged my legs apart, but then he realized he was still clothed—and he wasn't wearing Viking pants that were easy to jerk down. He mumbled what I was sure was a swear word under his breath and let me go.

I pushed up on my elbows and watched as he tried to figure out the fastenings on his jeans. His cock bulged against the denim, and I bit my lip. A real Viking warrior in my bed. How lucky was I? He finally got them off, dragging the pants down his legs and the shirt over his head. I whistled at the full vision of his body and made a *come here* gesture with my hand.

He strolled over to me. This time he pushed apart my legs and slid between them, dipping his head to taste me. I fell back at the feel of his tongue on my sensitive places, shouting and hitting the bed with my hand. He swirled his tongue around, and I arched up toward him. "Yes," I gasped. "More of that."

Rubbing my sensitive nub with his thumb and pressing his fingers into my wetness, he raised his head and looked up at me, watching the waves of sensation roll over me, as he pushed me toward the cliff.

"Roar," I cried out, shuddering as I exploded, my eyes rolling back in my head.

He surged up, pressing his thickness to me, and waited for me to come back to myself. He amused himself with kissing and exploring my neck and my chest. My nerves jumped, ready for more.

When I met his eyes, he grinned. He thrust into me, stretching me to my limits. *Well-endowed Vikings indeed.* His rhythm sent me skyrocketing, pleasure wiping away my thoughts. I gripped his muscular forearms and met him thrust for thrust. The pressure built, words tumbling from my lips, "More. Harder. Faster. More."

He gave all of himself, hitting just the right spots. Stars danced before my eyes as we burst together, in blissful passion. *My mate. Mine.*

# 7

# Skarde

Birger and I sat on what Peppermint called a couch. She'd left us with the visions of people playing before our eyes. They seduced us, demanding our attention, and we probably would have been entranced if the sounds of Roar and her pleasure hadn't filled our ears.

I glanced over at Birger, and he met my gaze.

He shrugged. "You'll get your turn."

I frowned at him. "You think she's easy?"

"Naw," he said, with a grin. "She's our mate."

"How do you know?" I asked, adjusting my seat.

"All these years, bound by magic? You don't think we recognize it?"

"But mates are a beast-man thing."

He nodded. "I've met my fair share on the battlefield."

I frowned. I'd known my friends believed in magic, and they'd seen me do some, but to know of the supernatural creatures that inhabited our world? "You believe?"

"What's to believe? I've seen it with my own eyes." Birger laughed. "Besides, she changed from her bird form in the underworld."

"Yes, but—" I shook my head. It didn't really matter. They knew magic was real, so why would supernatural creatures be a stretch? Besides, we came from a world where gods walked among us. "Do you know what mates are?"

"She belongs to us, and we to her," he said.

I blinked. That was the gist of it, but how could he know that without the understanding of the magic? I fingered the chain around my neck. Not that I could say I understood anything more, really. I could do a few spells, tricks really like getting rid of a headache. I'd thought to grow in power by taking the gem that hid behind my pendant, but in the last thousand years, I'd never been able to tap into its magic. The joke was really on us. We'd taken it from Loki, and he'd cursed us for it. I'd never been able to use the power I'd coveted. With a grimace, I turned back to the visions that played on the box that Pepper called a "teevee". My lips twitched.

"Are those supposed to be people like us?" Birger asked, leaning forward.

"I think so," I said, chuckling. Men and women in odd leather clothes with big weapons ran around shouting at each other. "Is that really what they think of us?"

"No Norse man would shave his head!" He belly laughed, pointing at the screen.

"What did the Jarl do? They let him get away with that?" I asked.

Cries of passion came from the other room, and I focused on the drama in front of me. Even if we were mates, I didn't deserve Pepper. I wanted her. The musky smell of her and the perfect curves I'd held in my arms would have made me want to make her my own, even if the magic hadn't wound between us.

But I'd gotten us cursed, I'd damned my friends, and someone as sweet and wonderful as her—I didn't deserve that kind of happiness.

Ignoring the sounds, Birger and I kept calling out every crazy thing these Vikings did. These modern people didn't understand us at all. They thought they could wear tattoos and long hair and carry an ax and they were Vikings. Vikings had hearts and souls. We were warriors, yes, but we were also people.

I remembered the family I'd left behind in our village—my brother, his wife, and kids. Our parents had died long ago, so my older brother practically raised me. We had different mothers, and I'd gotten the magic from my mother's family, but it hadn't mattered. We'd been kin. He'd never have forgiven me for my disappearance. I'd been so power-hungry, I'd have done anything to get my hands on this stupid gem. And all it'd ever done for me was get me and my friends locked up for centuries. My brother and his family were long dead, I was sure.

I glanced at Birger. He'd left behind a little girl. Sure, his sister was raising her, but she'd been his and he'd been so proud to lift her on his shoulders when we'd come back from raiding. Her blonde hair had shone in the sunlight like a halo around her head, and she'd gripped his big hammer in her hand like she meant to use it.

Roar had been an only child. The only one of his mother's seven sickly children to survive. His father had put every one of them out into the wind to die, certain they would never survive our harsh life. But when Roar was born, his mother had begged and pleaded. His father had taken him out to the old stump, meaning to leave him as he'd left the others. But Roar had lived up to his name, roaring like the biggest polar bear, his lungs sounding so strong and mighty that his father scooped him up and brought him home.

The guilt of the families I'd destroyed rode heavily on my shoulders. I'd dragged them all into this, and yet they had been punished alongside me. I'd had to get my hands on this magic, once I'd known it was real, and in doing so, I'd doomed my friends and myself.

This was my one chance to save us. We needed to find Loki and get him to undo the curse. I'd do anything, give anything. He could lock me up again for another thousand years as long as he let them go free. I sighed. Even after all this time, I didn't know what he'd do. He was the master of trickery. He'd probably take the necklace and toss us back in the underworld anyway. But I had to try.

# 8

# Pepper

When the doorbell rang, I jumped up and yanked on my clothes. Roar lay spread-eagled on the bed, sleeping peacefully. I ran my hand through my hair, trying to straighten it, and went to get the pizza. I passed the hallway mirror. I looked okay. Here's hoping that the delivery guy wasn't a shifter and didn't smell the sex on me. My cheeks heated on my way to the door.

I opened the door and Jess grinned at me. Three pizzas were stacked on his arm, and he held a case of beer in his other hand. "I didn't order beer."

He chuckled. "Kari told me you'd need it."

I rolled my eyes. The last thing I needed was to get drunk, but I guess if I'd offered the Vikings water they'd have laughed at me. What else did they drink in their time? Milk? I imagined the three of them with milk mustaches, and I giggled.

"Are you going to sign for this or not?" Jess asked.

"Sure. Thanks." I signed and took them. Spinning back to the living room, I kicked the door closed and stumbled toward the couch. I dropped the boxes on my worn coffee table, and the guys barely looked up from the TV. Guess they were getting used to modern life quickly.

"Hey," I said, snapping my fingers. "Pizza."

"What?" Skarde asked, looking dazed as if I'd roused him from deep thought.

I frowned. Maybe I'd misjudged them. "Meat pies." I opened the case and pulled out a can, flipping the top. "And beer."

"Yum," Birger said, reaching for the can.

I handed it to him, and he downed it in one long gulp. I laughed. Vikings and frat boys—who knew they had so much in common?

"I like this," Birger said. "Another!"

I snorted and handed him another can. I opened the pizza box and showed them how to get a slice. Sitting down on my armchair, I watched them eat like they'd never seen food before. Did the food in the underworld taste real? Was it filling like regular food? I had so many questions.

Roar came out of the bedroom scratching his neck. He'd pulled on the jeans again but hadn't bothered with a shirt. His tattoos stopped at his shoulders, then it was just hairless muscled chest. I wanted to run my hands over it again as I had when we were making love. He stopped, and I met his eyes. They were scorching like he was thinking the same thing. My cheeks heated.

"Food?" Roar asked, dropping down onto the arm of my chair. He reached forward and took a slice of the pie.

"Yes," Birger said. He opened a beer can just like I had and offered it to Roar. "Drink."

Roar downed it and let out a full burp. The other guys laughed, and I shook my head. *Boys. In any century.*

Skarde ate along with them, but his shoulders were hunched

and his dark eyes were somber. I met his gaze and raised an eyebrow.

He gave me a half-hearted smile. "Thank you, Pepper."

My hands itched to touch him, wanting to give comfort like a shifter. I stood and walked around the couch, then massaged his shoulders. Worry was soaked into his muscles, but he held himself tight and didn't sink into my touch.

"What's the matter?" I asked.

"We need to find Loki," he said, squeezing his hands together. He was one big mass of nerves. "And we haven't much time."

I nodded even though he couldn't see me behind him. "We have to break the curse."

"You know gods," Roar said thoughtfully. "You know Hades. Isn't there someone who might know where Loki is?"

"Absolutely. Kari is our best bet. I'll message her." I went to get my purse off the coat hook, and then returned to the living room. After pulling out my phone, I sent a quick text to Kari. *Thanks for the beer.*

*Hope you're taking advantage of all that muscle,* she wrote back.

I snorted. *Yup.*

*About time, girl!*

Of course, that would be the first thing my friend thought of. To be honest, it'd been the first thing that came to my mind when she told me about her mates.

*We need to find Loki,* I typed. My stomach twisted in knots with worry for my Vikings. I'd only just found them. They couldn't go away again. I sighed. Kari had to have some idea where Loki was.

*That jerk?*

*Yeah, he's the only way to break the spell.* I crossed my fingers, my toes, and anything else I could think of. Kari was a goddess;

surely she had some secret god hotline.

*I don't know where he is.* <sad face emoji>

My heart sank. It couldn't just be easy, could it? *Does Hades? He says . . .*

I waited. Had she lost connection or something? What was going on? I glanced at the guys, who were eating and drinking beer, but they were subdued, knowing their fate hung in the balance. My mouth was dry. It felt like forever before Kari typed back.

*He says he's helped as much as he's able.*

*What the hell does that mean?* Anger bubbled through me. It wasn't that I didn't appreciate Hade's help. He had got the Vikings out on their temporary pass. Still, we needed Loki's location more than anything.

<eye roll emoji> *He's just Hades. Sorry, Pep.*

*Yeah.* I pursed my lips. *Work your wiles on him, and maybe . . .*

<laughing emoji> *Will do.*

I clicked off the phone and looked up to see three Vikings staring at me.

"What was that?" Roar said, making a typing motion with his fingers.

"Texting," I said with a smile.

He frowned. "Magic?"

I really needed to explain what technology was and how it worked at some point. The magic answer wasn't going to work forever, especially if they stayed here in the modern world. "I was asking Kari and Hades if they knew how to find Loki."

Skarde leaned forward, listening.

"Unfortunately, they don't know, or maybe they can't tell us—" I lifted my hands. "And I have no idea how to find Loki."

"He could be anywhere," Roar said.

Birger snarled, squeezing his beer can until it cracked.

"No," Skarde said, shaking his head. "We're not going to accept defeat before we even try. We found Loki before, we can find him again."

"How?" I asked, a hopeless knot settling in my stomach. Had I found my mates only to lose them again? Before I even got to know them?

Skarde stroked his beard. "We know some of his places, where we lived . . . before."

"Yeah, we found him then," Roar said.

"And tricked the trickster." Birger smiled, his exuberance shining through even now when things looked so bleak.

"You never did tell me what you did to make him curse you," I said, studying them thoughtfully. Their eyes all shied away from mine. Was it really so terrible? "What was it?"

Skarde's shoulders slumped, but he spoke, his voice tired. "It was my fault. I made them."

"I don't think you could force your friends into anything," I said. They were bonded, like brothers, and you'd expect that after so many years of captivity, but they each had their own strong opinions. I doubted they'd do anything they hadn't decided to do. I couldn't see any of my Vikings letting Mr. Mulligan yell at them and just standing there and taking it.

"I told you I was a chieftain," he said. "I have some small magic. I can send messages, clear headaches, make illusions, that sort of thing."

I reached out and took his hand in mine. I was here for them. Whatever they'd done, it had been a long time ago, and it was time to forgive and forget.

"But," he continued, "I always wanted more magic, stronger magic, and when I heard of the Stone of Kunna, I wanted it. I didn't think about what trouble it would cause, or even if I'd be able to use it. I talked my friends into going to get it with me."

Roar nodded. "But we went willingly. We wanted to help."

"I played Thor," Birger said as if it was a surprise. "And we snuck into the camp."

"Loki was entertaining some giants, and his brother's presence distracted everyone so we could sneak in and take the amulet." Skarde turned over the raven's eye pendant in his hands and showed me the glowing stone set into the back.

It was green like the deep forest but run through with a smoky black. I'd never seen anything like it. "What does it do?"

"They said it did everything," Skarde said. "That a man could rearrange time and space with it, but . . ."

My eyebrows knit together. "But what?"

"I couldn't make it work."

I blinked. All that? They'd pissed off a god for a stone that did nothing? "Why didn't you just give it back?"

"Because we hoped it would work," Roar said. "We hoped that we could get out of Loki's punishment if Skarde just studied the stone long enough, that he'd figure out how it worked."

There was a quiet, thoughtful side to Roar that I was just beginning to see. "Why didn't Loki just take it back?"

"The stone doesn't let anyone take it unwillingly," Skarde said. "We were only able to take it because it was in a box, not being held by anyone."

"And once you possess it," Roar said. "It is invisible to everyone else."

"But he could still curse you?" And how could I see it if only those who "owned" it could? Was it part of the whole mate thing?

"Yeah," Skarde said. "I think he thought he'd be able to

find us in the underworld. But Hades hates him, and Hel, his daughter, was mad at him for losing her present."

"Her pre—" I stopped. "You stole Loki's gift for his daughter?"

The guilt was written across their faces.

"Damn."

* * *

The only answer to my Vikings' predicament was to find Loki. The only place we knew he regularly hung out was the Vikings' old stomping grounds in Sweden. They were going home, although I didn't think it would be how they had imagined—not the trip or the destination. I grimaced and picked up my cell phone to call an old friend.

"Carla," I asked, cradling the phone to my ear.

"Pepper!" she exclaimed, smacking gum.

Carla had always said she'd be Spearmint if her mom had named her after her favorite candy. At least she liked the flavor. I never went near anything peppermint tasting if I could help it. Caramel or chocolate, yeah, I was all over that. I swiped the imaginary drool off my lip thinking of Candela's cupcakes. I was stalling, mentally and physically.

"How are ya?" Carla asked. I could hear the mail shuffling in the background. Carla and I had trained at the same Post Office when we first started. We'd spent almost all our time together those first few years, but I'd been bad at keeping up since I moved away.

"I'm good," I said, forcing a casual tone, but my friend wasn't buying any of it. I wished I wore jewelry or scarves because I desperately needed to fidget and I didn't have anything nearby.

"Who is he this time?" I could hear Carla's arched eyebrow in her words.

"What do you mean?" I asked, glancing over at my men. The Vikings were chowing on their pizza. I was glad I'd ordered a pie for each one because there wasn't going to be much left.

"You sound like that time you scratched my favorite CD."

"I told you to download the album," I said. Carla and I were into the same kind of music: metal. She was the one who had first introduced me to the Viking metal I liked to listen to so much. "Your car had a phone jack and everything."

"Then what do I own all these CDs for?" she asked with a laugh. I could hear her shuffling the envelopes. "You know, Tommy Crabtree still gets all the letters here. The girls really love that jerk."

"Of course they do," I said. "Who can resist a blond-haired, blue-eyed . . ." Remembering Roar pressing his lips to my core, I twitched. I was hoping we'd have time for a repeat performance.

"Exactly." Carla smacked her gum and waited. She knew I had something on my mind, but she was also patient. I always appreciated that about her.

"So," I began, chewing on my lip. "Your brother still doing those runs to the frozen north?"

"Yup. Complains about it to no end." She chuckled. "But, you know, I think he likes it."

I took a breath. "I need a trip." Carla and I had discovered early on that the Post Office went everywhere and if you made friends with the pilots—and Carla had always been good at making friends—we could always hitch a ride. Her brother had expanded our reach to the other mail services and overseas. That time we'd hitched to Paris just for New Year's Eve was still etched in my mind. We'd had French guys buying us drinks all night, and their only reward had been when we'd thrown up on their shoes.

"Is that all?" she asked with a chuckle. "You know Jimmy'd do anything for you. Flash him some tit, and he'd grovel at your feet."

"Can you set it up?" I asked, hoping I wouldn't have to show him my tits. Carla was sweet, but her brother had never been my type.

"Sure thing," she said. "When do you want to leave?"

"Tomorrow." We didn't have any time to waste. This was our only clue as to where Loki'd be, and we needed to get him this necklace and make him undo the curse.

"You don't play, do you?" Carla said.

"He still leaves bright and early?" I asked.

"Five A.M. and don't be late. Jimmy will have a conniption."

We'd have to leave now to make it there in time, but I needed to make it happen. "Sounds good."

"You better get in the car now," she said.

"I know. Thanks, Carla." I clicked the off button and walked over to the couch. "You guys ready for a little trip?"

* * *

When we climbed out of the car, it was nearing four A.M. It had taken me all night driving, while my three Vikings sang, to get there. At one point, Birger had fallen asleep and the other two made fun of his snoring, turning it into animal sounds for miles. The good thing was none of them minded riding in a car now. But I glanced at the hanger—who knew how they'd feel about an airplane?

"Shh!" I said. "Remember what I said. We have to sneak on

to the plane."

"How do we sneak onto a magic bird?" Skarde asked.

His words were slightly slurred because they'd insisted on bringing the beer and the pizza in the car. How they could eat their weight in food and drink gallons of beer and still stand relatively well was beyond me. I'd either have been vomiting or falling over, especially with miles of travel on top of it.

"Very quietly," Roar said. "SHHHHHH!!" He pressed his finger to his lips and spat out the sound.

I rolled my eyes. Maybe the beer had been a bad idea. "Come on."

We crossed the road. The sky was still dark, although the flash of lights from the planes and the signals cut through the darkness. We went around the children's playground, empty in the early morning, heading toward the main airfield. The guys had been making grunts and noises, so when it got weirdly silent, I looked behind me. They were gone! Oh no. What trouble could they have gotten into already?

After retracing my steps, I found them playing on the playground equipment. Birger was lying upside down on the slide, kicking his legs and singing a song about lusty maids. Skarde was trying to stand on the swing, but he kept slipping off. Roar tried to walk along the top of the monkey bars, like it was a balance beam, except his inebriated state made him dance back and forth, and my breath caught in my throat. "Don't fall," I whispered under my breath like a mother hen.

"The stars are beautiful," Roar said.

I ran forward and hissed, "Guys. We can't be late."

"Why does it keep moving?" Skarde backed away from the swing and dragged out his ax. Shouting a battle cry, he attacked the swing. The chains jangled loudly in the quiet morning.

I sighed and muttered, "Shh, we have to be quiet."

"Yeah, quiet, quiet all the way to magic bird," Skarde slurred.

Birger whacked his hand against the slide in time with his song, and it echoed across the space. "Lusty maid-s-s, lusty maid-s-s."

Why was his song in English? I couldn't imagine how he had learned it. I grimaced. Was our American beer somehow stronger than their alcohol? It didn't seem possible, but my guys were really drunk.

"Come on," I muttered, hurrying over to him and pulling on his arm. "Get up. Plenty of time to rest on the plane."

"Whoop!" Roar cried, leaping off the end of the monkey bars and landing in the soft mulch. He wobbled but stayed on his feet.

Relief coursed through me, and I growled, "We've got to go."

Birger leaned against me, his arm over my shoulder, nearly toppling me with his weight. "Pepper, you're so beautiful."

"Thanks a lot," I said and put on my best scolding mother's voice. "Roar, get your butt over here. You too, Skarde."

Reluctantly, they stumbled over to Birger and me. I pushed all of them on ahead of me toward the hangar. Who'd have thought they'd be distracted by a kid's playground of all things? Guess I'd have to keep a special eye on them when they were drinking. Who knew what fresh trouble they could get into?

The snow had melted back into brown piles, but there was still a nip in the air. I'd dressed warmly, and the guys had put their fur cloaks over their t-shirts, but I didn't know if it would be enough. Of course, all that alcohol they'd drunk would keep them warm for a while. I smirked, but it soon faded as worry ate away at me. I had packed a few changes of clothes for us in my backpack, but it wasn't enough to use for extra warmth. Jimmy flew a mail plane and the hold wasn't exactly temperature-controlled, although it did have pressure and air. The Vikings had assured me they'd be fine, though. They were used to frigid temperatures, and Skarde could summon some magical fire if it was necessary. I wasn't so sure. What if they burned up the plane we were flying in? *Shit.* This had been a bad idea.

Maybe I should have bought them regular tickets on a commercial flight. Jimmy would take me as a favor, but we'd have to sneak the Vikings into the hold with the mail. But I didn't have money for the four of us to fly, and being cramped in tiny seats with other passengers was liable to make the Vikings freak out. They wouldn't be allowed their weapons, they'd pick a fight, and we'd end up thrown off somewhere before we even made it to their homeland.

No, this was better. As tricky as it was. I hoped they didn't get us caught before we even got there. And as Kari had said in her text last night, there was no telling if Loki was where they thought he was. He could be anywhere in the world. But they'd insisted that they knew his hangouts, and it seemed like we had a good chance of catching him. Even if he traveled around, he'd have to stop by the old places eventually, wouldn't he? I mean, it must be lonely when those who worshipped you were long gone.

We slipped in through the back door of the hangar. Luckily, it was quiet this time of the morning, so there weren't many people about to gawk at the Vikings' weird appearance. Or maybe unluckily—I winced when Birger knocked over a bench, sending a wrench skidding across the room, the clang of its metal on the cement echoing. I motioned for them to hide behind the plane when Jimmy came around the nose.

"Who's there?" Carla's brother asked, peering at me. He had

the same dark hair as my friend, but he had a rough beard on his chin. "Pepper?"

"Hey, Jimmy," I said, jutting out my hip. The Vikings were scrambling into the open hold, letters slipping under them. I hoped they remembered my instructions: get in and get hidden. *Hurry, guys, hurry.*

Coming closer, Jimmy laid the charm on as he said, "How've you been?"

I rolled my eyes. He wasn't a bad guy, although sometimes he acted like a total sleaze, but Jimmy thought he had way more sex appeal than he did. I forced myself to bat my eyelashes and said, "I was hoping I could hitchhike."

"You're not really dressed for the frozen north," he said, his eyes tracing my low-cut neckline. "But I'd be happy to keep you warm."

"I brought my coat," I said, brightly reaching for my backpack and tripping over its handles.

Jimmy rushed forward, catching me. "Clumsy as ever," he said with a laugh.

My eyes darted to the Vikings, who'd stopped and were pulling out their weapons, their faces stormy. They stepped toward us. *No, no, no!* I glared at them and tried to telegraph my thoughts. *Keep going!* They seemed to hear me, because they let their hands fall, although they continued to watch Jimmy suspiciously.

"Yes, I am," I said, standing up and getting free of Jimmy's wandering hands. I'd felt the squeeze he gave my tit in passing, but I hoped the Vikings hadn't seen. Even though they weren't shifters, they seemed to be feeling some of the protective effects of mating or maybe that was just how Vikings were. I tried to wave them on, and they moved deeper into the hold. I sighed.

Jimmy picked up my backpack and noticed my waving. He glanced around. "Is there someone else here?"

"No, no," I said, lacing my arm in his and walking toward the front of the plane. "Come on. You don't want to be late."

He nodded. "The mail is always on time."

I chuckled. "Yup."

We climbed into the cabin and settled in our seats. Jimmy hit the button to close up the hold, and the door whined as it closed. I glanced out the window, hoping the Vikings had settled in and weren't too scared by all the technology.

Jimmy reached over and squeezed my knee, giving me a full-wattage smile. "It's nice to see you again, Pepper."

I forced myself to smile back. It was going to be a long ride.

# 9

# Birger

A mighty roar filled my ears, and I jumped to my feet, brandishing my weapon. Skarde and Roar were beside me. The metal around us trembled with vibrations as the sound increased. I looked everywhere, but there was no mighty beast.

"Where is it?" Roar asked.

I shook my head. I hit the wall with my hammer, and it shuddered, echoing back at us, but no beast emerged. "Are we in its belly?"

"Pepper said it was like the car," Skarde said. "A great sound to make it go."

"This is no bird," I cried.

"But it's the same sort of . . . technology." Skarde's mouth twisted as he said the unfamiliar word.

The floor under us moved, and we stumbled. Roar hit the wall, and Skarde knocked over a few boxes. We were moving forward, then the floor tilted upwards. "What's going on?"

"I think," Roar said, "the magic bird is taking off."

The bird jerked, and pressure built around us, throwing us

back against the wall. My skin tightened and I could barely breathe as we lifted. Something loud clanked, and I tried to lift my hammer, but the strange wind kept us immobile. What was this thing?

After several minutes, the floor leveled and we dropped onto it, gasping.

Looking queasy, Skarde sat up and asked, "Are you okay?"

"I'm fine." I sat up and instantly regretted it. The walls seemed to move around me. A sour taste filled the back of my throat. "I'm a Viking. I'm fine."

We got to our feet unsteadily. Roar met my eyes, then we glanced at Skarde, and grinned. We shouted a battle cry, raising our weapons. We were warriors, and even riding in a magic bird's stomach was just an adventure. Hell, at least we weren't stuck in the underworld anymore, where every day was the same and the landscape never changed, and here we had Peppermint. I smiled, seeing her gorgeous form in my mind. She'd looked so lovely in that red sweater.

But my mood soured. That man, the driver, had looked at her so lustily. She was our mate. He didn't get to do that. I didn't like it one bit. I also didn't like being stuck back here in the stomach while he was up there with her. My hand curled around my hammer, and I snarled, "This isn't right."

Roar and Skarde glanced at me. Their faces weren't any happier than I felt.

"The bird?" Roar asked.

"No," I muttered. "Our Pepper up there with him."

"There's nothing we can do," Skarde said, his face turned down.

Roar scowled.

The bird bumped like an old cart on a dirt road until it settled into its flight. Pepper had said we would fly to our homeland in a magic bird. But she'd also said it'd be cold and dangerous. We Vikings were used to cold and danger, but we weren't used to not being able to defend our women. "We have to do something."

"She's a shield-maiden," Roar said. "She can handle herself."

I scowled. "She shouldn't have to. We are here. We are armed. We are ready to do it."

"I could do a spell," Skarde said.

"She said it would get cold," Roar said, "very cold and we might need your magic to stay alive."

Standing, I looked at the boxes around us. They were flimsy and made of some light material that just pulled open. Inside was mostly papers and messages in different languages that I didn't understand. I growled in frustration and kicked one.

There'd been so many times in my life that I'd wished I more than looked like Thor, that I'd actually been him. Thor would have been able to use his hammer to find Loki, wherever he was. He would have been able to protect his woman.

I pulled out my hammer and swung it at the boxes, sending them shuddering into each other. She was ours, our mate. No one had the right to look at her like that driver had. Roar and Skarde were true friends—I knew that after one thousand years of captivity—but when they pulled out their weapons and attacked the mail with me, my heart gladdened. We were more than brothers-in-arms. We were mates to our shield-maiden, our Pepper.

73

# 10

# Pepper

I climbed down out of the cabin. Nine hours cramped into a tiny plane was bad enough, but nine hours fending off the advances of a man who didn't know the word "no" was worse. Going back, I was booking a commercial flight. Even it cost me a fortune and my Vikings fought with everyone on board, *this* wasn't worth it.

Jimmy pushed the button to open the cargo hold, and the machinery creaked as it opened. He yelped when the inside was revealed. The neatly stacked boxes were gone. The mail had been shredded as if a wild animal had gotten loose in there.

"What the fuck!" Jimmy exclaimed. He spun around and looked at me. "Did you see any animals get in?"

I shook my head. I couldn't help the laughter that bubbled within me, though I didn't dare let it out. For sure, I worked for the Post Office; I shouldn't want to see mail destroyed like that. What about the poor people waiting for their letters? Or . . . I stepped forward and peered at an open box of . . . fruitcake? I snorted.

Jimmy spun, pulling his phone from his pocket and calling

his boss. He was going to get reamed out, but I couldn't find it in me to feel sorry for him. Not after nine hours of groping and terrible flirting. The Vikings climbed out as soon as his back was turned. Roar grabbed a handful of fruitcake and shoved it in his mouth.

I raised an eyebrow.

"What?" he asked. "It's good."

They were filthy, covered in bits of paper and packing material, but they all had big grins on their faces like they'd had the time of their lives. "What were you thinking?" I hissed, trying to school my features. "Destroying the mail?"

They shrugged and followed me out the side door of the hangar, no hint of remorse in their features. Not that I was worried about it. Let Jimmy deal with it, and maybe it would keep him too busy to harass anyone else.

"I didn't like the way he looked at you," Birger said, sliding up beside me.

I smiled. "I can handle Jimmy."

"I know," he said, taking my hand and squeezing it. "But you shouldn't have to."

The others "mmhmm'd" in agreement. I stopped and looked around at them. "Why did you destroy the mail?"

"Because we couldn't destroy him," Roar said.

Skarde smiled, snapping his fingers. "But if you like . . ."

I laughed. I wasn't sure what he could do, but I didn't think I wanted to find out. "No, leave him alone. I think you've caused enough trouble for poor Jimmy tonight."

"Never enough trouble," Birger groused.

We walked toward town from the airfield. There was snow on the ground, and it was cold and dark, but with my men around me, I didn't feel cold.

\* \* \*

The town was small and quaint, but the Vikings still gazed around with wide eyes. I supposed it looked very different from their time. How were we going to find Loki's stomping grounds, when everything looked so strange to them? "Let's find a place to stay tonight, and we'll see about getting ourselves oriented in the morning."

There was a pub on the main road, and we stepped inside, enjoying the warmth after the chilly streets. Warm lights hung over the bar and a live band played beyond the dance floor. Some men at the bar called out to us like they knew us, and my Vikings shouted back.

"Do you understand them?" I asked, pulling on Skarde's arm.

"They greet us in the old language. Well, something like the old language."

I frowned, glancing around, but they seemed like normal people. Everyone wore modern clothes, although I didn't understand a word of their language. I realized that in all those hours with Jimmy, I hadn't asked him anything about where we were going. But apparently, we were close enough to where my Vikings had lived that the language was still somewhat similar. That was lucky.

I wondered how we even understood one another, and why I hadn't questioned this before. I figured, in the underworld, it had been because of the magic, but when Hades had brought them to earth, had he given them the English language too? He must have because, other than an odd word here and there, they understood me. I shook my head. Magic was a crazy thing.

We sat at the bar, still dusted in paper scraps, and Birger gestured for beer.

I tried to object, saying we only needed directions to a motel, but the bartender brought four brimming steins anyway. The beer smelled yeasty and strong, and I took a sip. Then I pulled over the bowl of nuts because I was going to need something in my stomach if we were going to drink. I didn't want to end up dancing on the bar again like with Kari. The nuts were fresh and salty on my tongue. *Yum.*

The Vikings pounded their drinks and asked for another.

I smiled and reached over the counter for a menu. At this rate, I was going to need more than peanuts. Fries might be good, and . . .

Roar took my hand and winked at me. I released the menu. He pulled me onto the dance floor, and we listened to the slow, romantic song.

"You know how to dance?" I asked.

He grabbed my hips and pulled me close to him, rocking us together. "What's to know?"

Birger came up behind us, wrapping his hands around my back, and I swayed between them. Warmth uncurled in my stomach, my bird singing at being so close to my mates. Roar kissed me, and Birger nibbled on my neck. I sighed and glanced over at the bar. Skarde sat watching us, his gaze scalding. I gestured for him to come, and he shook his head, turning to his beer.

We danced through several more songs, then returned to our drinks.

"You could have joined us," I said to Skarde.

He just looked at his drink.

I kissed him on the forehead. "They don't blame you, you know."

His eyes lifted. "They should. I destroyed their lives and their families and everything good—for my greed."

"We'll give Loki back the pendant, and he'll set you free. Then it will all be okay."

"It will never be okay, Pepper," he said, sadly. "I will live with this guilt for the rest of my life."

I squeezed his arm, and he stood and walked away. His shoulders slumped.

"He'll come around," Roar said, sliding his arm around me. "The evil stone affects him more than he thinks."

The people Skarde passed leaned away from him as if they could smell the stink of the foul magic. "We need to get it away from him."

"He won't let it go," Birger said, on my other side. "He thinks it's his punishment to carry it until we can give it back."

"Do you guys still blame him?" I asked.

"No," Roar said. "We never did."

Birger grunted in agreement. "We went into this with our eyes wide open. We knew the dangers."

I kissed his cheek. "You are a good friend."

"What about me?" Roar asked, and I kissed him too.

The bartender leaned over the counter and said in heavily accented English, "You want me to call a cab?"

I nodded. "That'd be great. Where's the nearest motel?"

\* \* \*

The motel wasn't fancy, but it had a hot shower and a bed and that's all I needed. Too much travel in too short a time had wiped me out. I dropped my backpack on one of the beds and went straight to the bathroom, stripping and climbing into the shower. The hot water felt fantastic, and I scrubbed and scrubbed until I got every last bit of dirt off. Grabbing the thick robe on the back of the door, I dried my hair and ran a brush through it.

When I came out, Roar and Birger were asleep on one of the two beds and Skarde was sitting on the other. He stared straight ahead at the wood paneling as if he saw something I didn't.

I went over and sat next to him. "What are you looking at?"

He glanced at me, frowning. "Nothing."

"Skarde," I said, laying my hand on top of his. "We're going to get you out. For good."

"If we find Loki if there's a way to undo the curse." He scratched his beard. "If Loki will . . ."

"We'll make him," I said. "You are my mates. I'm not going to leave you trapped in the underworld." I looked into his brown eyes, full of so much pain and hurt, and my heart squeezed.

"What if all this is a trick?" Skarde asked. "Some way to get our hopes up before dashing them again?"

"We haven't even seen Loki yet. Are you going to give up so easily?"

"He could just keep me," Skarde said. "If he let Birger and Roar go, he could keep me forever."

"No, he couldn't," I said. I reached for the pendant, pulling it over his head.

He reached for my hands to stop me but didn't, and as soon as it was free, I tossed it across the room.

"Why did you do that?" he asked.

"Because the magic has been poisoning you for too long. You deserve one night without it."

"It's not gone," he said.

I wrapped my arms around him and held him to me. "It's gone for now."

We fell asleep like that, just holding one another.

*  *  *

The next morning we went down the street to a restaurant and got some breakfast. I had never seen a stack of pancakes as high as the one that Birger devoured. I paid with a card and decided to worry about paying it back later. What I was doing was more important than money.

I didn't know how we were going to find where we were going. I got a couple of maps and spread them out in front of the guys, but they couldn't make heads or tails of it. They just didn't see the world that way. I grimaced. "Well, what do you remember about the place?"

They started explaining it to me in terms of landmarks—rocks and woods and waterways that might not even be there after all this time.

"You mean the lake?" a young man said, leaning over the back of our booth.

The guys grumbled, but I put out a hand. "Do you know the area?"

"Sure," he said. "It's near Krampan. I hike a lot around there."

"Could you show us the way?" I asked.

He glanced at his watch. "Sure, I got some time this afternoon."

"Just point us in the right direction, then," I said.

"You in a hurry?"

"Kinda."

"Well, I'm going up to my dad's store. It's about halfway there, and"—he looked us up and down—"you all might need

80

some gear, going out there this time of year."

I winced, thinking of my poor credit card. "Sounds good. Do you think we can catch a ride from there?"

"Absolutely. Hikers come through all the time."

I beckoned the waitress and paid our bill, then gulped down the last of my coffee. We followed our new friend out to the parking lot. "What's your name?"

"Nils."

"I'm Pepper, and this is Skarde, Birger, and Roar." I pointed the guys out as I named them.

Nils laughed as he climbed into a four-wheeler and we all piled in after him, the guys in the back while I sat up front with Nils.

"What's funny?" Birger asked.

Our guide turned on the engine. "I've heard those names before, is all. I'm not sure where. They sound very . . ." He glanced at the guys' grim expressions. ". . . traditional."

"Yeah," I said, smiling brightly at Nils. "We Americans sometimes take the heritage a little too seriously."

He ran a hand through his blond hair and chuckled. "You'll like my grandmother, then. She's always talking about the past as if it was right in front of her."

"Yeah," I said thoughtfully. "We might want to talk to your grandmother." We'd never meet anyone who was as old as the Vikings, but even the previous generation might have some additional knowledge. One never knew.

"Well, she's at the store most days, so you'll probably see her." He turned up a snowy road, and trees replaced the buildings that had surrounded us in town.

The land was so beautiful and natural here, I could almost imagine it during my Vikings' time. I glanced back at them, and they stared out the windows as if they were starving and the very air was food. They'd been around so much modern life, new technology, and so many towns, they hadn't really had a chance to miss home. I bet this landscape made them feel sad about it.

After some time, we pulled up to a wooden store with a big porch. There were two wooden rocking chairs, laid with blankets, and lanterns hung along the roof. It looked a bit kitschy like it had been set up for tourists. We climbed out of the car and followed Nils inside.

"Hey, Dad," he said and waved an older gentleman over. His father looked just like him—tall and blond and well built. He introduced us, and his father nodded in greeting. "He doesn't speak English as well as I do, but he understands most of what you say."

His father smiled.

"Nice to meet you," I said, and the guys nodded in greeting.

Nils' dad glanced around at them, and he stopped at Birger, stepping forward. "Thor," he said firmly.

"Yeah, he looks like Thor," I said with a smile. "But his name's Birger."

The older man frowned. "Birger?"

I nodded.

He spoke in rapid Swedish to his son, whose eyes widened. Then he gestured toward the back room, and Nils ran off.

The guys' hands slid to their weapons, but I shook my head, waving them off. Something was wrong, and I didn't know what, but they didn't need to slaughter this innocent family.

A woman came out from the back room. She wore a knitted shawl and moved slowly with age. Her hair was white, shot through with a few strands of her original blonde. She looked up at us, her blue eyes running over each of us until they fell on Birger. Her breath caught in her throat as she studied him.

The Vikings had let go of their weapons at the sight of the old woman, but they all tensed. They looked like a bunch of misbehaving children under her wizen old gaze.

"Fadir," she said, stepping forward.

# 11

# Birger

I stared at the old woman. Her face looked so familiar, but I couldn't place it, like a dream I had seen long ago. Then she said the word, *father*, in the old tongue and I heard it on my baby girl's lips again. I stepped forward, sweeping her into my arms and holding her. I traced the lines on her face and looked into her blue eyes. "Inge! Great Odin. How is this possible?"

She stroked the side of my face, and then she hauled back and slapped me. I almost dropped her with the shock of it. Eying her warily, I set her back on her feet. I glanced at Skarde and Roar, who were looking at her with the same wonder I felt. How could my daughter, who was eight when I was cursed, be alive now, a thousand years later?

"What's going on?" Pepper said.

I couldn't turn my eyes away from Inge. She looked like my grandmother, but I could see the spark of my daughter in her eyes. "This is my child."

"That's not possible," Pepper said, leaning against the countertop.

Skarde stepped forward, speaking words of magic, and Inge spat at him. Roar crossed his arms over his chest, his face disbelieving.

But I knew my child. "Tell me how this is possible."

Inge turned and walked into the back room, and we all followed on her heels. She sat in a wooden chair that rocked with her motion and reached for a steaming cup.

I obsessively followed her every motion, seeing Inge, seeing my wife who died when Inge was one, seeing my parents . . . so much history in one body and somehow miraculously she was here. My heart beat against my chest, and I just wanted to take her in my arms, but she kept glaring at me. To be honest, my late wife used to look at me in the same way. "So like your mother."

She scowled at me and sipped from her cup.

"Tell us," Skarde said. "How did it happen?"

Inge glared at him even more darkly than she was looking at me. "Loki didn't think punishing you was enough."

I felt like a sword had run me through. This was a punishment. Loki had kept her alive as a cruelty. How could that be? "But you're here."

"I'm here," she said. "I'm a thousand years old and trapped in this ancient body for all this time."

Pepper gasped, and Roar pulled her against him.

"You've lived all this time," Skarde said slowly.

She coughed. "As a human with every ache, every pain that could be visited on a body. Dependent on the generosity of family to care for me, for generations."

"But you're alive—" My heart wrenched. My child tortured because of what I'd done? How could Loki do this to her?

"I just want to die," she said. "Maybe now Loki will let

me. Now that you're here to give that damn thing back." She gestured to the pendant around Skarde's neck.

I stumbled, my legs falling out beneath me. My daughter! Tears filled my eyes as pain wracked me. The whole world disappeared, and it was only me and her. The pain she'd been put through in my name pierced me to the core.

"Birger," Skarde said, his hand shaking my shoulder. "Birger."

"It's your fault," I said, shoving him away.

He came back, grabbing my arm, and Roar grasped my other one. They pulled me back to my feet and dragged me from the building. I fell in the snow outside, weeping and tearing at my hair. I'd destroyed my child's life. It was all my fault.

Roar squatted down in front of me. "Birger. Calm down, man."

"My child!"

"It's not real. She's not real."

"What are you talking about?" I cried out, shoving him away again. "You saw her. I saw her!"

Pepper wrapped her arms around me, and I wept, letting her rock me.

# 12

## Pepper

I just held Birger. No one came out from the store. Nils and his dad left us alone. The woman, whatever she'd been, hadn't followed either. Birger seemed to think she was his child, but Skarde was convinced otherwise.

"What happened?" I asked when Birger had stilled against me.

"Hel was teasing us," Skarde said.

"She really wasn't my Inge?" Birger asked, the lingering horror in his voice.

"No," Skarde said, inching closer, his eyes wary. "Inge wouldn't have been able to see the amulet."

I frowned. "But I see the amulet."

"You're our mate," Roar said. "You're connected to us."

"So, no one else can see it?" I asked. "Or no one human?"

"Only us, our mate, and Hel," Skarde said with a sigh. "Loki can't even see it."

"But why her?"

"Because it was a gift for her. Its magic is linked to her. That's why I could never use it."

"That's nuts," I said.

"How could she look so like my daughter?" Birger said, his voice unsure.

"She's a goddess. There are a great many things she can do," Roar said. "And her realm is the dead."

"She lives in the underworld," I said, understanding. "Why couldn't she just come and take the gem? You were there for so long. Couldn't she have resolved this?"

The Vikings shook their heads.

I stood up, reaching for the amulet. "Let's take it back in there right now and give it to her. Then this whole thing ends."

"It was taken from Loki," Skarde said. "He is the only one who can lift the curse."

"But it's hers, right?" I said. "She has this psychic link to the thing?"

They nodded.

"But it has to be gifted by Loki to her," Skarde said.

I rolled my eyes. These crazy rules. No wonder Kari was always complaining about her insane life as a goddess. I'd always known there had to be a reason I preferred being a shifter. All I had to do was get this curse undone, and my Vikings and I wouldn't have to put up with any more godly madness. I grimaced. "Wait! Loki can't see it?"

"No."

"Can he see you guys?" This was starting to make a whole lot less sense. We were hunting someone all over the world who couldn't even see us? "Are you hidden from him?"

They shrugged.

"We don't know," Skarde said.

"It was odd," Birger said, getting to his feet, "that he never came to the underworld to find us, to bargain for the amulet back." He rubbed his head. "Not once in all that time."

We'd been searching for someone who might not even be able to find us? I didn't know what Loki looked like—well, other than movies and shows, which looking at Birger, might be accurate. But still, he was the god of trickery—couldn't he be anyone or anything? "He can transform?"

"Yeah," Roar said. "Into anything. I mean, there's the legend of how he became a mare to lure away a great stallion."

The others smiled at the familiar story.

"And he became pregnant with his own foal."

My head spun towards Roar. "But isn't he male?"

Roar shrugged. "He's Loki."

I blinked. I so did not want to know how that happened. But if he could be anyone or anything, how were we ever going to find him? I turned back toward the store.

"Where are you going?" Skarde asked.

"Hel must know where he is. I'm going to ask her." I started forward. "Besides, she needs to answer for being an asshat to Birger."

"An asshat?" Roar asked.

Birger's arms came around me, and he held me fast. "You're amazing and strong, little one, but she'll rip you in two."

"But—"

"We'll find another way." He nodded and turned us toward the road. "That mountain in the distance, that's where we found Loki the last time."

"But it's miles and miles," I said. "And we didn't get any gear or supplies."

The guys laughed.

"We're Vikings, little one," Birger said. "We're used to surviving the elements."

They pulled their furs closer and started walking up the road. Birger wrapped his arm around me and led me after them. The road was packed with snow, but it wasn't hard to walk on. We'd bought clothing for the elements, if not supplies. My Vikings had their weapons and their intimate knowledge of the area. We walked until I didn't think I could walk anymore.

"Turn bird," Birger said, patting his chest. "You can rest against me."

"I'm fragile as a bird."

He grinned. "Don't worry, Pepper. I will keep you safe."

"You're not tired."

"We'll stop when we find meat and cook dinner; you can shift back then."

I nodded, letting my human form go and taking my cardinal form. I flew up to Birger, and he tucked me gently inside his furs.

\* \* \*

It seemed like hours later when Roar came back from scouting with a handful of rabbits. The guys made a fire and cooked them. I shifted back and lingered near the fire, enjoying the extra warmth. The sun went down, and the even greater cold descended on us. The nature preserve around was empty of human presence, so I could almost imagine we were back in the time of the Vikings. A thousand years later and the Vikings slipped into their old roles easily and comfortably. They'd built the fire near a rocky outcropping that kept the worst of the wind off us.

We ate, and my men told stories from their hunting days about bringing down the biggest elk or bear. They started to tell me about the raids, but honestly, I didn't want to know. They had lived such brutal, hard lives. How would they ever fit into modern society? It wasn't like going back to the underworld was an option. We would find a way to break the curse. But so much had changed, they were going to have a rough time of it. Good thing I was here to show them the way.

And here, in the middle of nowhere, I was grateful for every skill they had. They'd fed, entertained, and kept us warm. I couldn't really ask for anything more. I just hoped that Loki really was where they thought, that we hadn't come all this way for nothing.

They softened the hard ground by piling some brush as close to the fire as we could, and we snuggled in a puppy pile, using body heat to stay warm. My bird sang within me, so grateful to have her mates close.

When Birger leaned over and kissed me, heat erupted in my gut. I wanted them so much. My hormones flamed every time they came near, and here we were, freezing our asses off in the middle of nowhere. My hands ran down his body, seeking the places where his clothing parted to feel his bare skin. Roar was close on one side, and Skarde on the other. I reached for them both, wanting more. Roar took my hand and ran feather strokes across it.

Skarde stood and stomped away to the fire.

I opened my mouth to call him back, but Roar pressed his lips to mine. His fingers swept over my shoulders and down my arms, finding every crevice and memorizing my body. After our time at the apartment, you'd think he knew all the parts of me, but it was like he was discovering every bit anew. His hands played along my skin, over and under my clothes. His kisses trailed down my neck and up to nibble on my ears. He found my

91

favorite spot, the little inch just behind my lobe, and blew on it. I shook, need coursing through me. I didn't know what it was about that spot, but it did me in every time.

I reached for them, stroking their arms, their legs, whatever I could reach. Roar's cock pressed against his jeans, and I ran my hands along it. He groaned, throwing his head back. I smiled, enjoying my effect on them.

Birger undid the fastenings on my pants and slid his fingers into my wetness. I gasped. He rubbed my sensitive nub with his thumb, and I licked my lips. My body opened for them, not wanting to deny my mates anything. Electricity skidded under my skin. I opened my mouth to beg for more, but no words escaped.

When I was wet and ready for him, Birger flipped me over. My pants were pulled down just far enough to give him entry, and he covered my skin with his, but I wasn't cold anymore. He thrust inside, bigger and harder than Roar, if that was even possible, and I felt him stretch my insides. His position pushed him right up against my sensitive spot, and I cried out as he bumped it.

I reached out for Roar, not wanting to leave him out, and grasped his hard member. I stroked its length, and he pressed it to my lips. Eagerly, I took him in. Birger thrust inside me, and I gasped, taking Roar deeper. Both men moaned. Our rhythm was easy and immediate, as we took and gave joy in equal measure. We rode the rapids on the ocean, rising and falling as one. When the big wave came, it crashed into us all with such force that we fractured, merging and separating as the bliss raced through us.

My body slumped to the ground, and my men curled around me. Sweaty and tired, we closed our eyes, ready to sleep.

I opened mine a crack, looking toward the fire. Skarde sat slumped, the cares of the world riding his shoulders.

* * *

The terrain started to climb as we got closer to the mountain, but the Vikings kept trudging along. All the unspoiled nature really was beautiful. We'd gotten started early in the morning, and the colors changed as the sun rose in the sky. Winter birds called to one another across the treetops.

There were no cardinals on this side of the world, but plenty of others: twites, snow buntings, and artic redpolls. Mom and I hadn't traveled much. To be honest there hadn't been money for it. But seeing all this made me wish I had. I should have called her, but I doubted my cell phone would work here. She was probably wondering what happened to me since I hadn't called her back.

The tall trees gave way to rocky climbs as we went higher. I alternated between walking and riding with Birger on the way up. The rocks were piled against one another, making strange passageways and balanced tunnels.

"You know where we're going?" I asked, turning and looking back down the path.

Roar laughed. "This is our country. We know it all."

"It hasn't changed in all these years?" I asked.

He shook his head. "Nope. In fact—" He ran over to a clump of rocks just off the path and dug under them, his hands soon filthy. He pulled out a couple of small bags.

We all came over to see what he'd uncovered.

Roar dumped them out into his hands—three small carved wooden figures.

"Ha!" Birger exclaimed. "I knew you'd stolen them."

Skarde laughed. I didn't think I'd seen him even crack a smile before. Then he said, "All this time, you hid them here?"

"What are they?" I asked.

Roar chuckled. "Game pieces. We'd been playing on a board." He tried to gesture to explain what he meant, but I waved at him to stop, grinning.

"A board game, like chess?"

They shrugged at me.

I reached for one of the figures. "So, these are the pieces." I looked around. "But not all of them?"

Skarde snickered.

"Nope," Birger said, punching Roar in the shoulder. "This jerk stole them when he saw he was going to lose."

Roar scratched his neck. "I just didn't want you to be embarrassed when you lost again!"

Skarde was laughing so hard that he was holding his side.

I couldn't help staring at him. This was what it took for Mr. Serious to laugh. About time.

Roar dropped the pieces back in the bags and tossed them to Birger and Skarde. "To old times, my friends."

"To old times," they echoed, patting each other on the back.

We continued up the mountain. The Vikings helped each other when it got steep, using their skills in concert, as old friends did. I appreciated how bonded they already were, and yet they seemed willing to make room for me in their circle. Even though I didn't have the same strengths, they respected me too. I didn't think I'd ever felt anything like it. I was always fighting to prove myself as a person, as a human being, and having to stand there while my mother, my boss, whoever the flavor of the week was, yelled at me like I was a kid. I was tired of it. But these men treated me differently, even though I was a woman, even though they didn't know me that well yet. They treated me with respect. Was it because women could be warriors? Could be equals in their culture? Or was it because of the mate bond?

I reached for a spindly tree along the path, using it to drag myself upwards, and a loud crack echoed overhead. Skarde reached out, grabbing me and yanking me back. An *oof* escaped my lips, and I blinked at the tree I'd been reaching for. It was black and steaming, split down the middle as if struck by lightning. But the sky above was blue and clear. "I don't see any storms."

The Vikings pulled their weapons, their eyes searching for the source.

"I bring my own storm," a voice said from up the path. A tall, handsome, blond man strode toward us, spinning a hammer around in his hand.

The Vikings clustered around me, ready to defend.

"Thor?" I asked.

He grinned. "Glad someone knows the difference between me and . . . a fake." He eyed Birger, then he swung his hammer toward him, stopping just short of his head. "Loki?"

"No!" I cried out, hurrying toward Birger.

Birger lifted his hammer, ready to fight back. They were mirror images of each other, except for the lightning that crackled around Thor.

"He's not Loki," I said, wrapping my arms around my mate. "He just looks like you."

"Something Loki would do," Thor muttered.

"No lightning," I said. "Look, he's got no magic around him."

Thor tilted his head and dropped his hammer to the ground. "Huh. A doppelganger. That's pretty rare."

"Yes," I said.

"The last one I saw was over a thousand years ago," Thor mused, rubbing his beard.

He'd seen Birger? When they took the amulet or before? I cast my gaze around, but my guys didn't say anything. They were silent as if I knew how to talk to gods. Well, I had some experience with Hades and Kari. I bit my lip, turning back to Thor. "We're actually looking for your brother."

He scowled. "What do you want with him?"

"He's cursed my . . . er . . . friends here, and we want him to undo the curse."

Shaking his head, he said, "That's unlikely."

That we were looking for him? Or that he'd undo the curse? Gesturing to the mountain, I asked, "Is he here?"

Thor shook his head. "Nope. I've been kicking around here for a while, you know, with the giants."

I glanced around uneasily. "The giants?"

He chuckled. "Didn't your Viking friends tell you this was the giants' homeland?"

Shooting a glare at my men, I then asked Thor, "Do you know where Loki is?"

"Nope," he said. "Last I heard, he was off to some place called Spring Silver? Or was that Silver Springs?"

I gaped at him. We'd come all this way, and Loki was back home? No! That was crazy. Why hadn't Kari or Hades known he was there? I spun to my men. "We have to go back."

"But you've only just arrived," Thor said. "Don't you want to come to meet my friends?"

Behind him, two of the larger rock piles stood up, and I realized they weren't rock piles. Taller than houses, the giants wore the minimum of clothing and carried huge logs in their hands like bats. They grunted and lifted their weapons.

"They remember what happened last time you lot visited," Thor said with a shrug.

I blinked. "They remember these Vikings."

"Giants never forget a theft." Thor raised his hammer.

Birger grabbed me, tossing me over his shoulder, and ran back down the hill. Roar followed on our heels, and Skarde stood in the giant's path.

"No, Skarde!" I exclaimed, beating my fists against Birger's back. "He's going to get killed."

Skarde lifted his amulet above his head, turning the gem side toward them. A green light shone toward the giants, blinding them. Their bats crashed into the rocks and sent them tumbling after us.

Birger and Roar had slowed, avoiding the larger ones.

"He's just slowing them down," Roar said.

Skarde was running after us, and the giants were hitting everywhere, trying to find us. They knocked down several scraggly trees and sent more rocks tumbling toward us. The rocks seemed to be getting bigger and bigger the more they crashed around. We kept moving, but my eyes were on the hillside.

"They're going to cause an avalanche."

"I know," Birger said. "We need to find cover."

"On it," Roar said, he darted in ever-widening circles around us.

Birger kept moving but slowed down as the exertion got to him.

"I need to shift," I said. "Relieve the weight from you."

He just grunted.

Skarde caught up to us, faster without my added weight. That was my sign, so I shifted into my bird form. My perch on Birger's shoulder was unsteady, and I took flight, bobbing awkwardly next to them.

"This way," Roar called from down below us and to the right. We ran for him, dodging and leaping over the bigger and bigger stones.

Skarde tripped, slamming into a sapling. Then a larger stone slammed into him.

Birger and Roar took shelter in the small overhang Roar had found. They reached for me, but I avoided their hands, flying back to Skarde. He lay against the wood, blood seeping from his temple.

I chirped at him. *Come on. You can't stay here.*

He groaned, batting me away. "Go. Be safe, little bird."

*No. You have to come.* I pecked at his skin, trying to poke him awake. Taking the necklace rope in my beak, I pulled on it.

Skarde shook his head. More rocks careened past us, and the ground shook.

I shifted back to human, and I took Skarde's hand in mine. "Come."

He stared at me with wide eyes. "Back to bird, back to bird! It's not safe."

"Not for you either," I said, helping him to his feet.

A full-sized boulder crashed toward us, and Skarde whispered a word. The boulder turned, rolling away. Putting his arm over my shoulder, we hurry-limped to the overhang and climbed inside. The rocks continued to pound the land around us, but we stayed still and quiet and hoped the giants would tire of their game. They couldn't see where we were hidden so far down the mountain now, and maybe they would think we'd gotten away. Thor seemed to have tired of it because there weren't any lightning strikes among the boulders now.

We huddled together and waited. If we died here, at least we were together. Maybe years from now, Loki would find his pendant hidden here in the dirt.

# 13

## Roar

We huddled under the overhang, cowering like deer. I hated it. It wasn't how Vikings were supposed to be, but we had Pepper now. She was more fragile than we were, and this modern world was full of dangers. *Hell.* Even our old world had dangers enough, and trouble followed us wherever we went. And even the gods seemed determined to meddle wherever they could. What had we done to Thor? At least Hel had a reason to dislike us—for stealing her trinket. He must have just been helping the giants defend their domain. The gods had always been close with them.

We'd come so far, but there was nothing here. I grimaced. Loki was back in Pepper's town, and we only had a few days to find him and break the curse. Our shield brother, Skarde, had only gotten more morose so close to old memories. I had been glad to make him laugh with our old toys. And Birger, well, seeing that image of his daughter had hurt him even more than he showed. He buzzed with an aching pain that just made me want to smash things.

My mouth twisted. We needed to get Pepper home. Whatever

happened to us, she didn't belong here in this cold place. And we didn't belong anywhere. Our home was no more. Everyone we knew was dead, and we didn't fit in this modern world at all. Nothing made any sense.

Now I was sounding like Skarde. I needed to keep the faith. We'd find Loki and get him to break the curse. Then we'd make our home with Pepper and, somehow, we'd figure out a way to be in this new world. I scratched my neck. My tattoos were my reminder of the past, but I needed to look toward the future now. The future that we could have with Pepper if only we found a way out of this. I squeezed her hand.

She'd pressed snow to Skarde's wound, washing away the blood. It wasn't very deep; he'd be fine. But we'd all known what he'd tried to do back there—sacrifice himself for us. He blamed himself for the curse, for everything, but it wasn't his fault. Sure, he'd come up with the idea, but we'd all gone along. We'd been eager for adventure back then—anything new and exciting.

The rock falls stopped. I listened, but all seemed quiet. I shifted so I could look, but Pepper wouldn't let my hand go.

"It's okay," I said, unwinding her fingers and sliding my hand free. "I'll scout and make sure it's safe."

I stood slowly, looking over the edge of the overhang. I studied the rocks and the saplings. I couldn't see Thor or the Giants anymore. I moved out farther, willing them to move, to betray their presence, but nothing. Apparently, we'd bored them because they were gone.

"Come on," I said.

The others climbed out, silently. All around us lay pebbles and rocks of various sizes. The saplings that had dotted the landscape bent over, some knocked completely down, others bending under the assault.

"I don't think we're wanted here," Birger said.

"And our prey is in Silver Springs." Skarde wiped his hand across his brow, and it came away bloody and coated in grime.

Pepper nodded, her face determined. "Then we've got to find a way home."

We turned as a group and hiked back down into the valley. The trip was faster, now that we were familiar with the path, but we walked in silence anyway. We'd come so far and failed. Time was running out.

# 14

## Pepper

We passed the Nils' family store, and Birger shuddered. I patted his shoulder, and we kept going. On the main road, it got busier and some trucks passed us. It was going to be a long walk back to town.

I put out my thumb, hoping it really was the universal sign for "can I have a ride?" and that the armed Vikings with me wouldn't be too much of a deterrent. Swedes were apparently braver than most Americans because it only took a couple of vehicles passing before a truck pulled over for us.

An older man got out of the cab and gestured toward the truck bed. Half of it was stacked with firewood, and we climbed in next to it. I guessed there weren't many places to go around here, because before long we were back in town. We returned to the motel, and my red backpack, our only luggage, was on the counter.

"Wasn't sure you were coming back," the manager said, eying our appearance. We were covered in mud and blood and looking much the worse for wear. He grimaced.

"Yeah," I said coughing up a smile. "We got a little lost

hiking."

"Happens." He said that, but he didn't sound as if he was convinced.

"Can we get another room?" I asked, pulling out my wallet and my card. I frowned at it, knowing this trip was costing me a fortune.

The manager rang us up.

"Where's the nearest international airport?" I asked.

He told us, even describing where to go for the local flight to get there, and said he could call a taxi for us whenever we wanted. The manager seemed ready to do it right now.

We left the office, and I wondered what had soured him on us. Just our appearance or had Nils maybe spoken to him. It was a pretty small town. I bet they all knew each other. I guessed we should be grateful that we were being given a chance to clean up before getting a swift boot in the ass.

The guys brought in our bags, and I went straight to the shower, just as I had the last time. The hot water felt even more divine. I closed my eyes and let it just run over me, washing away the grime and the tiredness. Then I felt eyes on me, and I looked up. Outside the glass shower door, Skarde stood, watching me. I pushed open the door.

"Wanna join me?"

He grunted, but he didn't move.

I grabbed the bar of soap and ran it along my arms. "Then, what?"

"Why'd you come after me?" he asked.

"Because you're my mate."

He scowled. His eyes trailed over my skin as if he wanted to eat me alive, but he didn't move. "I didn't deserve it."

I blinked. "Deserve what? Saving? Living? Being loved?"

104

"You don't love me," he muttered.

"Fuck you," I said. "You don't get to tell me what to feel."

His eyes widened. "I doomed my friends to a thousand years of torture."

"They chose to be by your side."

He snarled, "We lost our entire families."

"All of you outlived your families," I said. "But you didn't lose them. Even after you were gone, they still loved you."

He was silent. His shoulders slumped, the red gash still bright on his head. "How would you know?"

I smiled gently. "I'm a cardinal shifter. That means I'm also a messenger to the dead." I rinsed the soap off my arms.

"That's how you came to the underworld. How you answered our call."

Grabbing a washcloth, I wet it under the water. "The living write letters to the dead all the time. They tell them how much they miss and love them, and I deliver those messages."

"Do they ever write letters of hate? Of how much they were disappointed?" He rubbed his knuckles against his beard.

"No." I stepped out the door and lifted the washcloth to his head. Gently, I washed away the blood and the mud.

"Why not?" he asked, his gaze meeting mine. His eyes were hurricanes of pain and heartache.

"Because they don't," I said, wiping down the sides of his face and across his lips. Then I stood on my tiptoes and kissed him.

He stood frozen for a moment, then his arms came around me and he kissed me back. All the hunger that had been in his eyes came out in his kiss as if a dam had burst. I drowned in him and he drowned in me.

I tugged off his shirt and undid the buttons on his jeans. He shed them, and I tugged him into the shower with me. The hot water pounded against our bodies. I traced the muscles and scars from his shoulders to the vibrating hardness of his cock. When I wrapped my hands around it, he keened, throwing his head back. I stroked him and watched the sensations rip through him.

For too long, he'd denied himself happiness and pleasure. I took my time, using the rough washcloth to clean him from top to bottom as if I could scrub away his pain. He groaned, reaching for me, but I turned him toward the wall, washing his back and his ass. I was patient, showing him how much I cared for him in every touch. When I finished, I let him turn and take me in his arms again. His hands roved my body, tweaking and caressing in turn, until every inch came alive for him.

He lifted me up, and I wrapped my legs around his waist. When he entered me, we both cried out. Each thrust of our merging made me moan anew. Heat swirled inside me as we rose to new heights. He closed his eyes.

"Skarde," I said, gripping his shoulders as he pounded me.

His eyes stayed closed.

I said his name again. "Be here with me."

"Pepper," he whispered, meeting my eyes.

I smiled, and I pulled him with me into orgasm. The water washed away the world, and we found each other in that empty space. For that moment of pure passion, we were all that there was—just me and him. No history, no curse, no heartache.

\* \* \*

We slept like the dead, and early the next morning got ready to go to the airport. I still had no idea how we were going to get the Vikings or their weapons on a commercial flight, but I figured we'd burned the bridges with Jimmy, and he was the only other option we had. "We'll have to pack the weapons for underneath."

"No way," Birger said. He sat on the bed, clutching his hammer to his chest. "I'm not giving her up."

I gave him a sidelong glance. "Does *she* have a name?"

Roar chortled, and I glared at him. He raised his hands innocently. "Hey, I don't name my weapons."

Skarde came in rubbing his reddish hair with a towel. My eyes traveled over his smooth skin, and part of me wanted to push him back into the shower for another round of what we did yesterday. I licked my lips.

He looked up. "This should be good."

"What?" I asked, distractedly.

Skarde grinned. "Birger telling you what he named his hammer."

My gaze skated back to Birger. "Oh yeah?"

"It's not so bad in our tongue," Birger said.

"But I'll think it's bad?" I asked, hands on my hips. How bad could it be?

Birger's gaze fell to the carpet.

I tapped my foot. "Tell me."

"In our language her name is Fitte," he said, his face hopeful that I wouldn't ask more questions.

"And in American English?" I asked. It was really amazing how much the leftover magic that clung to them had helped their translation skills. They hadn't forgotten their language, but they understood even slang in English.

"Her name is Wet Grass."

Skarde snorted. "Be honest. Her name is Cunt."

I scowled at them while trying to hold back my laughter. The image of him using Cunt to smack down his enemies made me snort. I couldn't believe Birger had named his hammer that. Kari was going to love this one. She'd roll and roll. Finally, my humor won out, and I burst into giggles. Roar and Skarde followed me, and Birger just stared at us.

"You're not offended?" he asked.

I leaned over and kissed his head. "No, I'm not offended."

Skarde went to our bags and started dressing. He pulled a blue t-shirt over his head, and then asked, "You were trying to figure out where to put weapons?"

I nodded. "Regular flights don't allow passengers to carry weapons on board."

"What do they allow them to carry?" he asked, pulling out his jeans.

My gaze stuck to his ass as he removed the towel, and I suddenly wished the motel manager hadn't called for a taxi so soon. "Um . . ." I swallowed. "The usual stuff: laptops, purses, or maybe. . . I don't know . . . instruments."

He glanced over at me, a smile curving his lips. "Instruments?"

"Yeah, I guess, if they were, like, in a band," I said. "They might carry their more valuable instruments on board with them."

"What would these instruments look like?" he asked casually.

Birger and Roar watched him curiously, and I wondered too—what was he thinking? I picked up my phone and looked up an album cover for my favorite Viking metal band. I laughed at how similar the band members looked to my real Vikings: same long hair and tattoos and clothing. I enlarged the image and handed it over to Skarde. "Like this."

"Hum," he said. "Put the weapons on the bed."

Roar dropped his spear and Skarde's ax next to each other on the bedspread. Birger clutched his hammer, then sighed and laid her gently next to the other two. Skarde padded over to the bed on bare feet and stretched his hand out over the weapons. He murmured some words.

The spear became drum sticks, the ax became a guitar, and Cunt transformed into a bass guitar. I blinked at how real they appeared. I'd known Skarde could do magic, but I'd never seen him do anything this big before. I ran my hand along the guitar. "The illusion will hold?"

"For a day or two at least," he said.

Birger whimpered.

I grinned. Maybe this was going to be easier than I imagined, and I had my own Viking rock band right here. I bit my lip. "We need papers. Can you create something out of nothing?"

"No," he said, shaking his head.

"Hum." I grabbed my phone and flipped through the images. I pulled up some pictures of passports, and then I grabbed the pad of paper from the nightstand. I tore off several sheets and laid them on the bed. "Can you make these into this? With our pictures and names on them?"

Skarde frowned and then held out his hands. He murmured some more words I didn't understand, and the papers twisted, trying to become what I had shown him. They were misshapen and strange looking. "Is this right?" he asked.

"Not exactly," I said, but I gathered them up anyway. Maybe we could find a real one that he could use as a model when we got to the airport.

"What music do these make?" Roar asked.

I pulled up a video of one of the bands, grateful for the hotel's

Wi-Fi, and handed it to him so he could see the instruments in action. Birger leaned in to watch with him while I packed up the rest of our stuff, and Skarde finished getting dressed.

The taxi arrived outside our door right on time. We all climbed in, and we were on our way. I glanced back, and the motel manager watched us from his doorway. Just making sure we left, I supposed.

Once this was all over and my Vikings were safe, I wanted to come back to this place and explore. This was where they'd made their homes all that time ago, and I thought these places would always hold a bit of their souls.

# 15

## Skarde

Pepper had convinced me to lay down the amulet while we were in the motel. I hadn't realized what a weight that thing was around my neck until I had to put it back on. My magic worked better than it had in years, without Hel's gem working against it. I felt free.

But then the car had come, and we'd had to go, and I hadn't really trusted it off my body. What if someone stole it and we had nothing to give Loki in exchange for our freedom? I couldn't live with that. I didn't want my friends to suffer any more for what I'd done, and I was even starting to think that I could forgive myself once we were free. That we might be able to have a new life with our mate, in this new world.

I sighed. It was all too good to be true. She was too good to be true. It scared me to even think of opening up to her, but when she'd pulled me into the shower, she'd been so perfect. She'd been my everything. I didn't even mind that I had to share her. Birger and Roar were my oldest friends. They'd been through everything with me.

The car pulled up to a large building, and we got out. I hung the strap for the guitar across my chest and picked up the bag for Pepper. We needed to find these papers she spoke of so we could get on the "commercial magic birds". I knew there was more to that story too. Pepper called everything magic, but I could feel no energies behind these things. They were human-made to appear like magic. Someday, she'd have to explain it to us, if we stayed, if we found a way out of this curse.

The building was bustling with people running back and forth and dragging bags behind themselves. A great roar filled the room as if from a giant ice bear, but these people didn't even flinch.

Pepper's hand came down on my arm. "Remember," she said. "That's just the magic bird. These are bigger than Jimmy's, and they carry more people."

We moved through the lines of people, waiting our turn to go to the counter. There Pepper had said we would purchase tickets for the voyage, and I should look for the papers called passports so I could fix the ones I'd magicked.

A child ran up to Birger and excitedly asked him if he was part of a band.

Birger smiled and squatted down to talk to the kid. On his back was what Pepper explained was a bass guitar and he pulled it around to let the child touch it. He was so good with children. I knew he'd have raised his daughter right, and I hated that he'd lost the chance. But here, watching him with this child, I considered that maybe someday he'd have another opportunity. Maybe we could make this work.

A woman in the line ahead of us caught my eye. She was flipping through one of the booklets. I leaned as close as I could, peering over her shoulder and studying the details. It should be easy enough to mimic. I reached for Pepper's backpack and pulled out the three attempts I'd made. Murmuring quietly, I passed my hand over them until they looked like the one the woman held.

Pepper held her hand out, and she flipped through them, nodding. "These should pass. Thank you."

I smiled. She always appreciated what I did and never took me for granted. Maybe if our village had done the same, I wouldn't have felt the need to go out and prove myself by stealing from Loki. So many regrets swirled within me, but I wanted to try to set it right. No, I needed to set it right. No matter what it took.

# 16

## Pepper

Skarde's magicked passports passed muster, and we soon had our tickets and were climbing aboard the small commuter plane for the first leg of our journey. This was the easier part. There were only twenty or so people aboard, and while the Vikings complained about the leg room and the view, they seemed relatively happy. People continued to stop and ask them about their instruments, and they gave more and more elaborate answers. I had to laugh over that. I bought some earbuds so I could play some of the music I had on my phone for them. Skarde scowled, saying it sounded like howling dogs, but Roar really got into it, banging his drumsticks against the tray table until I had to tell him to hush.

When the cart came around with drinks, I tried to suggest a soda, but they snorted at the bubbles and asked for beers instead. I sipped my Coke and looked out the window at the cold, clear blue sky. How could Loki have been in Silver Springs and no one had known? How would we find him, and what would he say when we did? The more time I spent with my guys, the less I could imagine ever being without them. How would I survive without Birger's boisterous calls for "another," Roar's thoughtful consideration, or Skarde's passionate care? We were mated, and I knew that with mating came love, but I expected it to take some time to develop. I'd wanted their bodies from the first moment I'd seen them, but they were human and didn't understand the bond, not in the same way, so I'd tried to take it slow. I snorted. As if climbing on Birger right there in the cave had been slow. But I cared about each of them. More than I could have ever imagined.

The first plane ride was so easy that I expected the same for the second. We made it through inspection and climbed aboard the international flight. This one was packed in tighter, and the guys already had a few beers under their belts. My credit card bill was going to be astronomical when I got home, but at least we were on our way.

I'd gotten up to go to the bathroom once we were solidly in the air. The tiny space was barely enough room to do my business but somehow contained a mirror. I glanced in it, expecting to see dark circles under my eyes, but I looked happy, content almost. I grinned. I'd never imagined it, even a week ago.

A fog rose up behind me, and a face appeared alongside mine in the mirror. Her eyes were green and sharp, outlined with a smoky black and scowling at me. Her hair piled on her head was a mix of white and black, and when I turned to look, knowing there was no room in here with me, she had no body. "Who are you?"

"I'm Hel, little one," she said, her voice sickly sweet.

Loki's daughter. The one who'd abused poor Birger so much. "What do you want?" I muttered.

"Just that your Vikings should know who brings the horror."

"What do you mean?" I asked, frowning. "They've been

punished enough."

"They stole my present before I even got it," she growled.

"But they were held captive for one thousand years!"

"That was my father's punishment," she said with a cruel smile. "Not mine."

Then, as quickly as she'd appeared, she was gone. I hit the mirror with my hand. "It's not fair. They don't deserve your punishment. They want to give the damn thing back."

Terrified about what she'd done, I hurried back out into the cabin and looked around. Everyone seemed exactly the same, eating and drinking and listening to music. The woman on the aisle turned to me and raised her glass of wine. She opened her mouth to speak, and her jaw fell to the floor.

I screamed.

The other passengers turned to me, muttering. Their skin went gray, and bits of flesh fell from their bodies. The flight attendant turned toward me, reaching out her hands and muttering, "Brains."

*Zombies? Fucking zombies?* My gaze darted around looking for the Vikings. We'd gotten seats near the front of the plane, but I couldn't see them as passengers rose from their seats and tried to amble toward me. A commotion started along the aisle, and my Vikings came toward me, using their illusioned weapons to knock the zombies out of the way.

Birger raised his bass guitar, and I shouted, "Don't kill them! They're magicked."

"But they're attacking," Roar said, beating someone off with his drumsticks. He clipped the zombie's ear, and it flew across the cabin, landing with a smack against the windowpane.

"Ew," I said, then shook myself.

"What's going on?" Skarde asked as he beat back a passenger

with his own arm.

"It's Hel. She's cursed everyone on the plane," I said, shoving the flight attendant away from me. She stumbled, knocking into the passengers behind her and they all fell like dominos.

"Not everyone?" Skarde said, meeting my eyes.

"Oh, shit," I said, turning and running for the cockpit. The plane shifted as the nose dropped, and I fell more than walked toward the doors. I grabbed the handle and yanked on it, but it was locked.

"Here," Skarde said, coming up behind me. He passed his hand over the lock, and it clicked.

I shoved open the door and stared at the two pilots moaning in their seats. Skarde went in, banged their heads together, and shoved them back into the main cabin. We could still hear shouts from Birger and Roar battling the others. We dived into the cockpit, and Skarde pulled the door closed behind us. The plane was plummeting toward the ocean below.

"Can't you do something?" I asked.

He shook his head. "I don't understand this magic enough to manipulate it."

I groaned.

"But you're a bird," Skarde said. "Don't you know how to fly?"

"Yeah, but that's by instinct not technology. What even are all these knobs and buttons?"

"Didn't you say there were those safety things? Can't we use them and just jump?"

"And leave all these people to die?"

"But they're zombies!"

"They won't always be. Hel will change them back."

He looked at me in disbelief. "Hel did this? We're doomed."

"Well, thanks for that." I pushed more buttons, and they just yelled at me. What were we going to do?

Roar leaned his head in breathless. "You got this under control?"

I rolled my eyes at him. "Sure, all good here." Then I reached for the headset and mic that the pilot had dropped. I tapped it, listening to see if it still worked. "Mayday, mayday."

Roar hit someone and popped his head in again. "'Cause we need Skarde to stop the zombies."

I glanced at Skarde. "Can you do that?"

"I can try," he said.

"Go," I said, jerking my head toward the door. When it closed behind me, I sat down and tried to go through everything on the control panel. Something must work. But nothing did. Every button I pushed just flashed and did nothing. I tried the radio, but we were too far from land or Hel was blocking it. Either way, we really were doomed. We were going to die and take a whole plane full of innocent people with us. But even if we saved them, if they were in pieces, would they survive? What about the guy whose ear was mashed into the side of the cabin? I shuddered.

When Hel had tricked us before, it had been an illusion. She hadn't really been Birger's daughter. Could she be playing a trick on us with a plane full of zombies? Were we somehow not falling at all? I looked outside, and the clouds whipped past us. It certainly felt real. My stomach swirled uneasily.

I felt my pockets for my cell phone. There had to be someone I could call, but I'd left it back in my seat. I yanked open the door, but the cabin was chaos. A zombie slipped on someone's spilled drink and careened across, bumping into another who was trying to eat his neighbor's arm. The Vikings were hitting them with the blunt end of their weapons-slash- instruments and trying to at least slow them down, if not knock them out.

"Dammit," I said, swinging the door closed again behind me. "Loki, this is all your fault!"

A man appeared sitting in the co-pilot's chair, his legs crossed. He winked one sharp green eye at me. "Is it?"

*Holy fuck!* I stumbled back against the door. "Loki?"

"The one and only," he said with a grin.

His green eyes were so familiar. He'd been in Silver Springs, and I'd bumped into him on my way to the rink. But I hadn't known what he looked like. I swore. It didn't matter. I bit my lip. I wanted to go off about the Vikings and how he needed to save them and then the zombies and his daughter and all the things, but I blurted, "Can you stop the plane?"

He snapped his fingers. We froze in mid-air, not flying, not moving, just frozen in a nosedive position toward earth.

I took a breath. We were alive, which was more than I'd hoped for. "Can you stop the zombies?"

He stood up and crossed to the door. "May I?"

I nodded and scooted out of the way.

Loki opened the door and peered into the cabin. He whistled in appreciation and glanced back at me. "I don't think my daughter would take kindly to me messing with her spell."

"But she shouldn't have cast it!" I wanted to shake him.

He shrugged. "She does have a mind of her own."

"You punished the Vikings already!"

"I did," he said. "But she didn't."

I groaned. Gods and their crazy semantics! Why couldn't they ever just give me a straight answer? "You can't stop this?"

"I can't interfere with the spell," he said. "But I could . . ."

A grin spread across his face, and I really didn't like it. Loki was a trickster. Whatever he proposed wasn't going to be good.

"What?"

'Tsk tsk, Pepper, you really should be nicer to me." He crossed back over to the console and flicked a few more switches. "You are begging for your life here."

I swallowed. "Okay, what do you propose?"

He crossed his arms over his chest and raised an eyebrow.

"Oh great and mighty Loki," I intoned.

"I do love to hear that. I don't hear it much anymore." He chuckled. "So, little cardinal shifter, I propose that I will bring anyone from Silver Springs you think might help."

I ran the wording through my mind, trying to find any loopholes. "Anyone or anyones? Will you keep bringing people until the problem is fixed?"

"Sure," he said, but he lifted a finger. "But I cannot bring a god or goddess. Hel wouldn't like that."

No Kari or Hades. That sucked. But with all the supes and folks with special skills in Silver Springs, there had to be someone.

"At your leisure," he said, picking a bit of lint off his shirt.

I delivered mail in Silver Springs. I knew everyone in town, by name at least, but now that I needed a name, my mind was completely blank. After several minutes of additional crashes from the cabin, I blurted, "Storm."

Loki smiled and snapped his fingers.

I ran to the door and shoved it open.

Storm stood in the middle of the fight. She shifted into her raptor form and grabbed a nearby zombie to bite into his arm. Her body was so big that it took up most of the plane, squishing the fighters together. The zombies didn't care. They bit into whatever flesh was nearest—dead or undead.

"No! They can't be hurt," I cried as Storm ripped an arm off a male zombie. I needed someone else. Storm was too strong.

"No! Gray! I want Gray!"

Storm disappeared in a puff of smoke. In her place stood Gray.

"What the fuck?" Gray glanced around at the madness.

Without another word, she leaped into the air, throwing her legs around a zombie's neck, taking it to the ground. She extended her wolf fangs and bit into the zombie's arm. It looked like she was reaching around for something to use as a weapon, when I cried out, "No! They're humans!"

Loki grinned. He waved his hand, and Gray disappeared.

"Crap, no." I was getting these people hurt worse. I wracked my brain for someone who could do more. "Um . . . Zoe!"

Zoe appeared with a white fluffy pet in her arms. That must be Snowball, who I'd heard so much about.

I glanced at Loki.

He shrugged. "Two for one deal."

A zombie rushed at Zoe, and she flicked her wrist. He floated up like he was in space. He still kept reaching for her, but he couldn't get any traction. His fingers neared her, and Snowball snapped at them.

When faced with dozens of long, sharp teeth, even a zombie had enough self-preservation to retreat.

Zoe petted Snowball, and I think the thing actually purred.

This wasn't working. I needed someone with magic who could stop the zombies. Where was Skarde? I thought he'd been working on a spell. He was over against the wall, chanting, but nothing was happening.

Loki peered over my shoulder. "It's getting pretty messy out there. Your Vikings might get eaten soon."

My heart rose in my throat, and I scrambled for any name I could think of. "Lys!"

"Coffee?" Lys said, offering Loki a cup. She looked perfectly polished in her knee-length dress and bright red lipstick.

"Definitely," Loki said, taking it. "This summoning is thirsty work."

She turned to me, and I shook my head. Caffeine was the last thing I needed. My heart was racing as it was.

Loki waved his hand and sent Lys back.

I was getting desperate. This wasn't working. I needed some way to stall time so Skarde could figure out the spell.

"All done?" Loki asked.

"Jack!" I exclaimed.

Jack appeared as if he was in the midst of a conversation and gazed around at the zombies. "What in the frozen hells?"

Loki grinned. "This one might be fun."

One of them stumbled toward him and grabbed his arm. He threw them off and growled, "Don't touch me, or I will freeze your dingles off."

But that didn't stop the zombies, and as they kept coming, he sent out a wave of frost, freezing them all in place. Their poses were comical since they were all in the midst of attacking each other or the Vikings.

My gaze darted to the Vikings, frozen. "Let them go, Jack!"

"Which ones?" he asked.

"The big hairy ones," Loki said and sipped his coffee.

Jack snorted and pulled his ice back from Roar and Birger. Skarde still sat facing the wall, chanting. Somehow, the wave had missed him.

My gaze darted to Loki as I realized what he said. "You can see them?"

He shrugged. "Of course."

"Then why didn't you go to them in the underworld? And get your amulet back?"

Loki's eyes narrowed. "Hades makes that difficult."

*Good for Hades.* Loki needed someone to make his life difficult since he was so good at doing it for everyone else.

"I'd like to get off now," Jack called, and Loki obliged with a snap of his fingers.

Birger and Roar looked around, dazed, and then hurried over to me. They stopped when they saw who was behind me.

"Loki," they said.

"It is my name," he said, rolling his eyes.

"Do you remember us?" Roar asked.

Loki tilted his head and gave them a look. "The Viking that bears a remarkable resemblance to my brother? And his friends who stole my daughter's amulet? How could I forget?"

"You cursed us," Birger said.

"Well, duh," Loki said. "But I also sent this one to rescue you." He jerked a thumb at me.

"No you didn't," I said. "There was a letter and the magic rink . . ."

"Skates, actually," Loki said.

I scratched my head. "But Kari used those skates too. You didn't magic them for her."

Loki shrugged.

I was getting really tired of those shrugs. "So, you wanted me to get them out. Why? You cursed them there. Why not get them out yourself?"

"More fun this way," he said with a smile.

I didn't believe him for a second. There must have been some reason he couldn't get them out. But it didn't matter. He was here now. "You want the amulet back."

"Of course."

"Will you call off Hel?" I asked. "And land this damn plane?

123

And release the Vikings from the curse?"

"Demanding, isn't she?" Loki said to Roar and Birger. "But I do like a woman with a bit of fire."

I just glared at him. The Vikings stood silent and surprisingly patient, and the sound of Skarde's chants came to us. I wanted to run over and hug him, telling him he could stop, but I didn't trust Loki out of my sight.

Loki finished the coffee and set the cup on a nearby cart. "I guess I could get you out of this predicament."

"The plane, passengers, and crew on their way, none the wiser," I demanded. "And us returned to Silver Springs."

He grinned. "So feisty." Then he waved his hand, setting the cabin and its occupants to rights. With another snap of his fingers, we were all standing in Silver Springs by the ice rink.

It was quiet and dark. The zamboni ran over the ice. I gulped in the fresh air in relief. We were home. Roar, Birger, me, and . . .

Skarde appeared next to us. His eyes were wide and his voice hoarse as he said, "What happened? Where are we?" His eyes landed on the god. "Loki?"

"The plane's safe?" I asked. "And everyone aboard?"

Loki rolled his eyes. "Enjoying their drinks and watching the clouds pass by. Now, where's my amulet?"

"All in one piece?" I asked, remembering the ears and arms they'd lost.

He snorted. "Relatively."

"Hel won't come after us anymore?" I asked. I forced myself not to look at Skarde. I had forgotten that Loki couldn't see the necklace. "She seemed to think my Vikings deserved more punishment."

"No, once I have the amulet, she won't have any need to."

"That doesn't mean she won't," Roar said.

"Fine, fine," Loki said. "I'll make her stand down."

"And the curse?" I said, taking a breath. Things were finally going our way.

Loki shrugged that damn shrug again. "I'm afraid there's nothing I can do about that one."

Or maybe they weren't.

# 17

## Birger

We stared at Loki.

"But you're the one who cursed us," I exclaimed. Skarde's shoulders slumped, and Roar looked toward the ground. I knew what they were thinking because I was thinking the same thing. A thousand more years of captivity? How could we survive it? We wouldn't—that was the answer. We'd be insane. There was no way we'd survive being cooped up again, even if Pepper came to visit every day. Besides, we couldn't ask her to do that. It'd be like visiting the dead.

"Yeah, poor planning on my part," Loki said. "I was so angry that I didn't make an escape clause."

"Poor planning?" Pepper gasped, raising her fists. Roar pulled her into his arms and held her back. Our little bird was so fierce. It made a warrior's heart proud.

"Now," Loki said brightly, holding out his hand. "My amulet."

Skarde sighed and started to lift the string from his head.

"No!" I snarled. "If he can't give us our freedom, he doesn't deserve it."

"Birger," Skarde said. "It's his. We were wrong to take it in the first place."

"And it's not like it has ever done us any good," Roar said.

"You're better off without that foul magic," Pepper said, although there were tears in her eyes.

I shook my head violently. They were nuts. Why were they giving it to Loki when he couldn't even do what we needed?

Pepper reached out and placed her hand on my arm. "If you'd made a gift for your daughter and someone stole it . . ."

My heart sank. They were right. It was selfish. No matter what, we were doomed. We might as well give it back. I gestured to Skarde to go ahead. I wouldn't argue anymore.

He took the amulet off and handed it to Loki. As soon as Loki closed his hand around it, the necklace shimmered with power.

"Well, hello to you too," Loki crooned.

Roar snorted, and we all laughed. All this time, that thing had been no more than a lump of rock on Skarde's neck. It had never glowed or shimmered or shown any spark of magic in our possession. We'd risked everything for that damn rock and lost nearly everything, and it had never done us a damn bit of good.

Pepper squeezed my arm, and I glanced over at Skarde. He looked lighter and calmer than he had in a long time. Right there, that was worth giving the pendant back.

Loki tucked the amulet in his jacket and looked at us. The corner of his mouth twisted with what almost looked like regret. Then he disappeared into thin air.

"Let's go home," Pepper said.

Roar's stomach growled. "And order some pizza."

"And beer," I said with a smile. We needed to enjoy whatever time we had left in the real world, with Peppermint. When we went back to the underworld, we'd have to let her go. A beautiful woman like her shouldn't spend her time mourning a bunch of lost Vikings when she could be seeing real men in the real world.

My heart ached. But we were her mates. Could a beast-woman even survive without a mate? I didn't know. I wasn't sure we were going to survive without her.

We walked together into town. The sky was clear tonight—the crescent moon and the stars shining on the canopy—and it was beautiful. Even if it was one of our last nights on earth.

# 18

# Pepper

When we got back to my apartment, we sat around watching television like it was just a normal night. I was squished in between Birger and Roar, and Skarde sat in the armchair. If they'd been going to stay, I'd been thinking I needed to upgrade my furniture—get something sturdier and roomier. I didn't like my men not being in arm's reach. I also needed to order some food, but I didn't want to move. This might be our last time together, and I didn't want to waste a moment.

Because they weren't going to stay.

My Vikings were going back to the underworld. I tried to let that thought settle within me, but I wanted to fight back. There had to be a way to keep them on earth. Because if there wasn't, I didn't want to be here either. I crossed my arms over my chest and glared at the floor.

They were my mates. I could feel the connection humming between us, and I wanted to rip their clothes off even now. But more than the sex, I'd come to appreciate each one of them and why the fates or whatever had chosen them for me. I blinked.

That was it! We needed to go see the Fates.

I jumped up from the couch and hurried toward the kitchen. After grabbing my phone off the counter, I hit speed dial on Kari's number. I shouted in her ear when she answered, "KARI!"

"What is it, Pep?" she asked, a sleepy note in her voice.

I glanced at the time. It was something like two in the morning, but my friend wouldn't care. "I need your help, or rather Hades' help."

"Oh?" she asked. I could hear Hades' grumbling in the background. He appreciated his sleep more than most gods. "He says he can't uncurse them."

"The Fates!" I exclaimed.

"What the hell does she want with those miserable cows?" he grumbled loud enough that I could hear him.

"I have an idea. I think they could help."

"Hades said they don't help anyone but themselves."

"But it's our only chance," I said. "Loki says he can't undo the curse."

"Why, that little . . ." Kari's voice rose with her annoyance. I could hear Hades making soothing sounds in the background. "I'm fine, I'm fine."

"Kari," I began.

She was still muttering at Hades. "Yes, Loki is a shit. I don't care what you say."

Hades murmured.

"Well, if you can't undo it either, then you're just going to have to help my friend. I don't care how much the Fates annoy you. Get Pep and her guys there now."

More noises.

Then my living room disappeared, and the Vikings and I were

tumbling through space. I cried out, but my own voice just echoed back to me. We landed on a cave floor strewn with straw which didn't cushion our fall at all. I groaned, holding my back. Roar moaned, and Birger echoed him.

"I thought we had a few more days," Skarde said, gripping his head.

"You do," chorused three females.

I looked up blearily into the faces of a young woman, a middle-aged woman, and an old woman. "You must be the Fates."

"They are big, strong brutes," the old woman said, leaning over Birger and Roar. Her eyes fixated on the bulges in their pants. "Are they big all over, Peppermint?"

I swallowed. "Why, yes."

"How thrilling," the young woman said, clasping her hands together.

Birger blushed, and I snorted.

"Yes, they are," I said, wriggling my eyebrows.

The Fates laughed. Each one had their own unique sound, but they also blended in a weird harmonious way.

We climbed to our feet.

"Would you like something to drink?" the middle-aged one asked. "Tea, coffee. . . beer?"

The Vikings looked awkward like they'd just been caught with their hands in the cookie jar. But eventually, they spoke up.

"Yes, madam. Beer please, madam."

"This way, then," the young one said, almost floating toward the opening.

"No weapons allowed," the middle-aged one said sternly.

My men set their weapons down gently on the floor and tiptoed after the Fates. I followed and stopped in the doorway. The next room didn't look like a cave at all but like a cozy living room. There was an overstuffed couch and two armchairs in varying shades of pink and purple. The coffee table was glass, outlined in gold, and a tray holding several beers sat on it. The floor was covered with a gold and purple rug that looked like my feet would just sink into it, and tapestries of various scenes were hung on the walls. Across from us was a large, flat-screen television and the announcer called the wrestling match before one of the Fates turned down the volume.

"You watch wrestling?" I asked before I could stop myself.

The grandmother answered, "They're such big, virile men, don't you think?" Then she winked.

I chuckled.

"Sit, sit," the middle-aged one said, and the Vikings perched uneasily on the fluffy furniture. She handed each of them a beer.

Birger studied the wrestling show, and Roar leaned back on the cushions, trying to get comfortable.

The young one slid her arm through mine. "Now that the men are settled, let's us girls talk." She led me through into the next room.

Skarde started to rise, and the middle-aged one shooed him back.

"We'll take good care of her," the elderly one said.

The next room was a kitchen, shining white, with a small breakfast nook table. It was set with flowery placemats and next to a window that looked out over a green meadow.

I stared at the image. "That's not real, is it?"

"No, dearie," the middle-aged woman said, dropping into one of the oak chairs. "But the fiery pits of hell do get so tiresome."

The other two nodded their heads.

"Now sit down," the grandmother said, "and tell us how those

Vikings are in bed."

The middle-aged one rolled her eyes, and the youngest one leaned in closer.

"But I need to ask about—"

"We'll get to all that boring stuff later," the grandmother said. "Juicy bits first."

"Are they really hung like . . ." the youngest Fate asked, her face full of curiosity, "horses?"

They all looked at me expectantly.

"Well, yes," I said, and I thought they were going to get up and cheer.

"You don't think you'd let us borrow them?" the oldest asked. "Just for a night or two?"

I snarled, and they drew back. "Sorry," I said, holding up a hand. "They're my mates."

The middle-aged one nodded and patted my hand. "To be expected, my dear. Don't let these two horny biddies get to you."

"Thank you," I said, feeling like I had to give them something. "They are fantastic in bed. Roar does this thing with his breath on my earlobe . . ."

The Fates smiled knowingly.

"And they are all so big. I wasn't sure I'd be able to accommodate . . ." I blushed madly. It was one thing talking to a friend like Kari about this stuff, but I didn't even know these ladies.

The middle-aged one brought us all glasses of white wine, and I took a sip to be polite, but the last thing I needed to do was get drunk. Especially with so much riding on this conversation.

"Oh, do drink up, dearie," the grandmother said, draining her glass. "This wine is delicious."

I took a swallow. "So, about the curse?"

"A terrible, terrible thing," the middle-aged fate said, and the others nodded their heads. "It's like they were frozen in time."

"Knotted up all the string," the grandmother said, frowning.

"Frustrating," the young one said, sipping her wine delicately.

"Loki says he can't undo it," I said, watching them carefully.

"Turd," the grandmother said, chuckling.

"Of course he can't," the middle-aged one said. "There's only so much even gods can mess with the weave of the Fates."

"Can you undo it?" I asked, feeling like I was shoving my hand into a pool of sharks. They were as likely to bite it off as they were to help me. But this was what I'd come for and I wasn't going back until I had an answer.

"Knots like these are very bad," the young one said with a scowl.

"But," the grandmother said before upending another glass of wine, "fated mates will not be denied."

"Like the sleeping one who awoke to true love's kiss," the middle-aged one said, laying a finger by her nose.

"So, it can be undone?" I asked eagerly.

The youngest Fate smiled. "Of course."

"But," the grandmother said, holding up her glass, "not by us."

My eyebrows drew together, and I took a swallow of my wine. "Then by who?"

"That would be telling," the middle-aged one said.

The young one nodded.

*Dammit.* I drained my glass and held it out for more. Tears of frustration rose up in my eyes. My week was almost up. No one could help, and all the Fates could say was 'the power is inside you' like it was all some game. "I need them."

The Fates patted my shoulders.

"Remember the fairy tales," the grandmother said quietly.

The Fates sent us back to Silver Springs without a word more. The guys had really enjoyed the wrestling and decided to try a few moves on each other in the front yard of my apartment building. I sat on the step to watch their gymnastics and try to figure out the Fates' puzzle.

What did 'remember the fairy tales' mean? They'd mentioned Sleeping Beauty specifically, hadn't they? But the Vikings hadn't been sleeping when I found them, and we'd kissed enough to wake a million beauties. What was I supposed to do with this information? We needed to break the curse before it was too late. We didn't have time to play with riddles.

"Pepper," Roar said, dropping down next to me. "Don't worry."

"How can I not worry? We only have hours left!" My head fell to my hands. "I can't lose you."

"You're not losing us," Birger said, coming to stand in front of me. "You can come see us any time."

"Not that you should," Skarde said. "You should go on with your life."

"I can't just go on with my life! You're my mates." I looked up at them, memorizing their faces.

Roar wrapped his arms around me, and I leaned into his warmth.

"Do you guys know any fairytales?"

They looked perplexed.

"What is this word?" Skarde asked. "Tales we have of men and gods, but we don't know 'fairy.'"

"Why do you need to know?"

135

"It's what the Fates said." I sighed. "'Remember your fairytales.' They mentioned Sleeping Beauty, where the kiss of true love breaks the curse."

Birger leaned forward with his lips pursed, and I snorted. "We've kissed a million times."

"No harm in making it a million and one," Roar said, kissing my cheek.

Skarde took my hand and pulled me to my feet. He wrapped his arms around me and kissed me. Roar curved his hand around my ass and leaned in to kiss the back of my neck. Birger lifted my hand and kissed the palm. Warmth flooded through me.

"We're outside," I said, a little breathlessly.

"The best place for sex," Skarde said, undoing the buttons on my shirt and kissing the skin as it was revealed. "Have we ever told you how beautiful you are?"

"The neighbors," I said, trying to pull them toward the building and failing.

Birger leaned in, plundering my mouth, and my legs weakened.

Bracing me from behind, Roar continued to lick my earlobe and the tender space just behind it. He pulled my shirt off my shoulders and undid my bra.

"It's cold," I protested when Birger let me up for air.

"Then we're not doing our job." Skarde pulled my bra off and took my nipple in his mouth. He rolled it gently against his teeth, and I swallowed.

His arms wrapped around me from behind, Roars fingers made quick work of the fastenings on my jeans. They'd learned quickly these Vikings. He plunged them into my wet folds, and I moaned. The three of them stroked and teased me to a fever pitch right there on the porch of my apartment building. When

I thought I couldn't take another moment, Roar sank down behind me and Skarde's expert hands flipped me over.

Roar's cock stood tall and beautiful in front of me, and I leaned down to lick it. He trembled at my touch, and I grinned. Climbing up him, I licked my way to his mouth and kissed him. His hardness pressed against me. Gentle hands lifted me, and I slid myself down onto Roar, inch by inch. He moaned. Once he had filled me completely, I gasped and started moving. I'd never thought I'd be able to accommodate such size, but I seemed to expand to fit and it was all pleasure.

Hands roamed over my back and ass and pressed me forward. Cold jelly was rubbed in my asshole. I barely had time to think where that had come from when I felt Skarde press against its opening. "I can't," I said.

Skarde kissed my earlobe. "Magic, remember?" He pushed into me, and I groaned, but there was no pain.

I was full of my mates, and pressure built inside as we moved. I reached my hand out. "Birger."

He was there, pressing his dick to my lips. I took it inside instantly, wanting to feel so full. They took up a perfect rhythm, and we began to move as one. Three as one—I'd never dreamed it possible, but the mate bond pulsed between us, and pleasure radiated through me. We took and we gave all of ourselves, bonded mates who could no more live without one another than live without air. My limbs trembled as the build-up intensified, but they supported me—my fierce Vikings. When I came, sparks exploded through every inch of my body and my eyes rolled back in my head. The volcanic eruption roared through my body, through my soul, and shook the very world around me into a million pieces.

Afterward, the guys carried me upstairs and washed me gently in the tub. They tucked me into bed and snuggled around me. The four of us overloaded my queen mattress, and the bedsprings creaked. They slept, and I cried silent tears. This may well be our last night together. We'd kissed, and the curse wasn't broken. I'd lose my mates. For a shifter that was a fate worse than death. My body was sated, and my soul whole, but my heart broke with what was coming next.

* * *

Despite my fears, we woke late the next day. I opened my eyes and moved and stretched. The guys woke around me.

Roar leaned over to kiss me. "Good morning, sleepyhead."

I laughed. "And you all have been up partying?"

He grinned and trailed his fingers along my thigh.

"Hungry," Birger groaned.

The rest of us laughed, even Skarde who sat up scratching his beard.

"As much as I'd love to stay in bed with you all day," Skarde said with a wolfish grin, "We should probably get some food."

"Sounds good to me," Roar said.

"I guess we could order pizza." I looked around for my backpack. "I need my phone. It's in my backpack."

Skarde fetched it and brought it to me. I turned it on, staring at the messages downloading across the screen. Mom. Boss. Mom. Boss. Kari. Mom. Boss. We'd only been gone a couple of days. What in the world was going on?

"That's a lot of letters," Roar said, peering at the text messages.

I gave him a smile. "They're like letters. The phone sends them over long distances." I clicked through them. Mom and my boss were both pissed at me, but I didn't really want to deal with either of them. If my Vikings were going back to the underworld, I didn't want to waste a second to answer these messages.

Mom would understand. Mr. Mulligan not so much.

"They look very angry," Roar said.

"You can read them?" I asked, puzzled. Hades really had given them the whole package if they were able to read English too. I wondered if they could write. I should thank Hades. That was very kind.

"Why does this one called Boss say such mean things to you?" Roar asked.

"Because I haven't shown up for work at all this week."

"You called him, though," Skarde said. "I remember. You pretended to be sick."

I snorted. "Yeah, Mr. Mulligan would have expected me to call him again, though, unless I was in the hospital."

Birger shrugged. "What a jerk."

I shook my head. "No, he's a boss. He's doing what he's supposed to do by keeping track of his employees."

Roar growled. "I don't like how he talks to you. You shouldn't put up with that."

I looked at the messages again. "But I've ditched him all week."

Birger shook his head. "You told him you were sick. Doesn't he have anyone else to abuse?"

"Well," I said. "The other mail carriers usually cover for me. We all pull in for each other."

"Then why does he need to talk in all caps?" Roar asked.

I grimaced and echoed Birger's words, "He's a jerk."

"We should beat him for talking to our shield maiden like

139

this," Birger said, getting to his feet.

"Tie him up in some magical knots," Skarde said.

Roar held up a hand. "No, Pepper must stand up for herself. This is her battle."

The others looked thoughtful then nodded.

"What?" I said. "I can't stand up to Mr. Mulligan. I need this job. Especially after we decimated my credit card in Sweden."

"No, Roar's right," Skarde said. "You are strong. We know you can do it."

"If you let him stomp all over you," Birger said. "It will never end."

Roar squeezed my arm. "Do it, shieldmaiden."

I frowned at them, but they were right. I'd been letting Mr. Mulligan abuse me for too long. Sure, I liked my job, but I didn't need to be treated like this. I stood and grabbed my robe off the back of the door. Wrapping it around me, I took the phone out into the other room and dialed my boss.

# 19

## Roar

I was so proud of our mate, going to do battle with her boss. She was a true warrior. I rolled out of bed and pulled on my new clothes. When we went back to the underworld, would we return to wearing our wool and linen clothing? I'd actually started to like these jeans and found them more comfortable than our traditional clothing.

The door was cracked, and I could hear Pepper's quiet words. She was calm and respectful, but she told him that she didn't appreciate how he treated her. She told him she was taking the rest of the week off and when she returned on Monday, she expected better behavior. I snorted. She scolded him, but she never belittled or stooped to his level. It was perfect. She was perfect.

Birger groaned from the bed. "Hungry."

"We are too," Skarde said. "But we'll be fed soon enough."

I glanced over at them. "We should take Peppermint out to eat, like at that restaurant in the homeland."

"I'd rather order pizza," Birger said. "And stay in bed, and Pepper would too."

"That's exactly why we can't let her," Skarde said, giving me a nod.

"She's going to be sad soon," I said. "Let's take her out for some fun."

Birger nodded. "She needs to laugh. She's been too worried."

"Yes," Skarde said. "And it wouldn't hurt any of us either."

I raised an eyebrow at him. Getting rid of the amulet had done him so much good. He was back to his old self, well, as much as any of us could be with the future awaiting us. I'd hoped we could live out our lives here with Pepper, but the curse couldn't be lifted. "Have you thought of any fairytales?"

Skarde scowled. "I don't know. Did the Fates mean our tales or hers?"

"There are many old tales of curses and their cures," Birger said.

"But what would apply here?" I asked, scratching my chin. "Do we seek help from the gods? Or from some magic item?"

"No, that's what got us into this mess," Skarde said. "It has to be something like true love's kiss or forgiveness or something."

"We love her, and she loves us," Birger said, in his honesty saying aloud what we'd only been thinking.

"Maybe we need to say it aloud?" I asked. "I love Pepper."

"I love our little bird," Birger said.

Skarde said, "I love Peppermint."

"Well, I love you guys too," Pepper said from the doorway. "But what was that?"

We waited a moment, to see if we felt any different, but nothing changed. "Nothing," I said and jerked my head towards Birger. "He's hungry."

"Oh," she said. "I was going to order pizza, but they don't open until eleven."

142

"Let's go somewhere to eat and maybe dance," Birger said, wriggling his eyebrows.

Peppermint chuckled. "Guys, it's ten in the morning."

"What's your favorite place for breakfast?" I asked, reaching for her. We couldn't seem to get enough of touching her. Her skin was incredibly soft and smelled like honey.

"I don't want to go anywhere," she said. "I just want to go back to bed and lay there wrapped in your arms."

"Aren't you hungry?" Skarde asked.

"What food would cheer you up?" Birger asked.

She hesitated, looking at us, but then she nodded. "Candela's cupcakes. They're better than . . ." She gave a small smile. ". . . almost better than sex."

We laughed heartily. Nothing could be better than the sheer bliss of holding our mate in our arms and claiming her.

"Let's go, then," Birger said, holding out a hand to Pepper. She took it.

I nodded. "Let's go." We walked together, all of us finding some way to touch her and be close to her.

# 20

# Pepper

The ice rink was busy when we got there, people gliding perfectly across the ice. Must have been free skate time. I hadn't ever had much need to check the schedule since I came here so rarely, and I didn't skate. The Vikings were entranced by the skaters though.

"They're skating," Skarde said.

I leaned into him, enjoying his new lemon-musk scent since the amulet and its foul magic was gone. "Yeah, do you guys know what that is?"

"Yes," Birger said, a big grin on his face. "We love skating."

"What are they wearing on their feet?" Roar asked, tilting his head and peering at the skaters' feet.

"Where are their bones?" Skarde asked, his voice puzzled.

"Bones?" I asked, then shook my head. "They wear boots with blades on them."

"Oh," they said.

"After cupcakes, can we skate?" Birger asked, squeezing my hand.

"I'm terrible at it . . ." I trailed off at the expression on their faces.

Roar laughed. "We'll help. All shield maidens should know how to skate!"

Their excitement was infectious, so I reluctantly agreed, but this time I was getting a cupcake and hot cocoa first. We tromped down the street toward Candela's shop. My Vikings called out things they didn't recognize, and I tried to explain. I'd stopped using "magic" for everything, and I hadn't even realized. Well, if they were going to live in the modern world . . . except they weren't. My heart squeezed.

We tromped up to Candela's shop and almost ran into an older man on his way out. He wore a long fur coat and woolen boots. He carried a staff that was etched with symbols that seemed vaguely familiar. His gaze swept over me and the Vikings, and his eyes swirled white. "Returning to the magic pools, brothers?"

His voice sounded strange to my ears, almost sing-songy. I tried to focus on him, but he seemed to shift in and out of place. What was going on?

"Wanderer," the Vikings said, their voices full of awe.

"To wash away the curse, you must go to the magic pool," the stranger said.

"Where?" I asked, leaning forward. "What pool?"

The old man winked at me and gestured to the ice rink behind us. Then he shifted into a raven flying toward the sky.

"Odin," Skarde breathed.

The others nodded.

I blinked. I'd been visited by more gods in the last week than I ever had in my life. "Did he just say that the ice rink will break the curse?"

"I think so," Skarde said, glancing toward the ice. "But how are we supposed to 'wash away the curse' if it's frozen?"

We hurried over to the edge of the rink. The skating had made ridges in the ice, and pieces of it had flaked off. Birger leaned down and picked one up on his finger. He looked at all of us.

"It can't be that easy," I said, nearly holding my breath. Hope beat against my chest. I wasn't sure I could bear the disappointment if it didn't work.

Birger scrubbed the ice against his skin. The air around him moved, shuddering.

I licked my lips. It was probably so disgusting with all the people who had skated over it, and dirt and grime, but if it worked, I didn't really care.

Roar dragged off his furs and his t-shirt and reached for a chunk of ice. Without even glancing around to see who was looking, he rubbed his body with it. He didn't even shudder at the cold. The air moved around him too. Birger tore off his shirt, then reached for another chunk.

I spun to Skarde, who stood stock-still watching them. "Can you see it?"

He nodded. "The ice chips wash away the curse. The magic flows off of them."

Waving him forward, I said, "You too."

"I don't deserve it," he said, shaking his head.

"Like hell," I said, grabbing his arm and dragging him over to the rink. "You're mine, and I don't let what's mine get away."

He looked at me in surprise as if I hadn't told him every step of the way.

"They forgive you, Skarde," I whispered, leaning close to him. "It's time to let it go."

"But—"

I pressed a finger to his lips. "You've been punished enough."

He gazed at me and then nodded.

My heart warmed. We were going to be okay.

Skarde reached for a scoop of ice. He rubbed it up and down his arms until the hair stood on end.

I shivered just watching. Wrapping my arms around myself, I couldn't help but grin. The curse would be gone at last.

Birger unzipped his pants and started to push them down. I ran over and grabbed the waistband, looking back and forth at the other skaters. "I don't know if we need to go that far."

Skarde took off his shirt and washed his arms and chest. I swallowed.

"Odin said bathe," Roar said, dropping his jeans to the ground. He stood proud and naked. Birger chucked an ice chunk right at him. Roar caught it and rubbed it over his toned belly.

My eyes followed the little drips of water down into his navel. I fanned myself.

Someone snorted nearby, and I turned to see a blond man slapping his leg and laughing. I could see the flash of his tongue ring in his open mouth. He looked really familiar like I might have seen him before. Was he a stripper?

A blonde woman ran forward, snapping pictures. "This will make a great calendar," she said. "You guys don't mind if I snap some shots?"

"Shots of what?" Roar asked.

I imagined a calendar of the Vikings on my wall, and it didn't seem like a bad idea. The woman looked like a Viking herself, all blonde hair and blue eyes. But I shook myself and ran forward. "It's free skate, guys," I said. "No stripping on the ice."

"Aww, come on," another woman called, and there were several other boos and hisses from onlookers.

Scooping up Roar's clothes, I hurried over to him. "Put them on before you get arrested."

"What's that?" he asked, sliding a leg into his pants.

"They lock you up in a boring room for a long time," I said.

His eyes widened, and he yanked his pants on. But he didn't bother with a shirt, and I stood back, watching them wash away the magic. Warmth bubbled within me. My Vikings weren't bothered by the ice. In fact, if the pools hadn't been covered, they'd have probably dived into the chilly water.

I smiled. That was a nice word: mine. I was starting to think I'd get to keep my mates. I wondered what they'd do in this new world. There weren't battles to be fought and villages to be plundered. Would they be happy with a quiet life in Silver Springs?

Zoe walked by clutching her furball. A fire burst out on the top of one of the buildings, and Jack sent an ice wave over it. When had it ever been truly quiet in Silver Springs?

They scrubbed until Skarde didn't see the magic clinging to any of them anymore. I hugged them each in turn, unable to believe they were mine and we could now be together, here on earth.

Looping my arm through Skarde's, I turned toward Candela's shop again. "This calls for a real celebration."

We barged in and up to the counter.

Candela came forward to greet us and raised an eyebrow at the exuberant Vikings behind me. "What can I get for you?"

"Beer," Birger called, slapping the small table.

I chuckled and said, "A dozen caramel cupcakes and four large hot chocolates."

"Are you sure it'll be enough for them?" she asked with a small smile.

"Frankly, no," I said, "But it's a start."

The guys sat in the pretty pink chairs, and they looked ungainly and oversized. At least we were the only ones in the shop. I glanced around and saw the husky at the end of the counter. He gave me a dog laugh, and I snorted.

"Here you go." Candela set the cupcakes on the counter. Her red hair was tied back in a ponytail.

I took the tray over to the guys and set it down. They were staying. The curse was over. I could hardly believe it myself.

Birger reached for a cupcake, and I swatted his hand. "Save one, or maybe two for me. Don't eat them all."

They nodded in agreement.

I turned back to the counter, and Candela had put up our hot cocoas. I lifted them and turned back toward our table. I must have spun too fast because, in classic Peppermint fashion, I tripped, falling toward the floor. Only, Roar dived forward and caught me.

"Thanks," I said, giving him a peck on the lips.

The shop was strangely quiet. I turned to see what had happened and found the drinks floating in the air. Skarde winked at me as he made them float over to the table. Thank goodness for supernaturals. Then I bit my lip and looked toward Candela.

I'd thought she was human, but she stared right at the floating cups, a frown creasing her forehead.

"Give me a minute," I said to Roar, and I approached Candela with a smile. I had no idea why the barrier spell hadn't worked, or if she even knew what she had seen, but I supposed I ought to find out. "Candela?"

Her eyes darted to my face. "Did you see that? They floated."

"Yeah," I said with a forced laugh. "Must have been a trick of the light . . ."

"Don't lie to me," Candela said.

Something in her voice made me say, "I won't," and I meant it. She obviously knew about the supernatural somehow, and it wouldn't help to keep lying to her.

"I came to Silver Springs for answers," she said.

"Why?" I asked, curiosity getting the best of me. Silver Springs might be full of supernaturals, but it didn't mean they were likely to spill any secrets. The town was warded so that humans shouldn't even see the magic, but it didn't work for everyone. My Vikings were a prime example.

"Because this weird stuff started happening around me," she said, rubbing her arms. "I don't understand it yet, but I know the answer is here in this town."

"You might be right," I said with a shrug.

"I'm human, at least I thought I was," she said. "But these strange . . . I don't know."

"You'll figure it out," I said, leaning over the counter and patting her arm.

"Do you really think so?"

"I do," I said. There was a strength and determination in Candela, and it would see her through.

"Thanks." She lifted her chin toward the Vikings. "They're quite rowdy."

"They just got their lives back," I said with a grin. "It's allowed."

Candela smiled back at me.

She deserved all the help she could get in figuring out her life. I didn't know if getting a mate or three would help, but it had certainly made my life richer. I couldn't imagine ever being without my Vikings. "You might try the rental skates with the green splash on them. I mean if you skate . . ."

She nodded. "I might. Thank you."

I headed back over to my men. The cocoa and the cupcakes were delicious as usual. Rich and chocolatey mixed with caramel yumminess, it really was the perfect food. I could live on it. I ate my fill, and I couldn't be more content, here in one of my favorite places with my mates.

Feeling way too pleasantly warm after cupcakes and hot cocoa, I took the guys to rent ice skates. They eagerly handed over their boots to the attendant, thrilled to try out the new kind of footwear. They didn't even complain that someone else might have worn them as they had at the thrift store. We laced on our skates, and they glided out over the ice. They were amazing. Despite their size, my Vikings were elegant as dancers. They had no trouble figuring out how to make the blades work, even though they must have been so different from the bones they'd used. They reached for me, ready to bring me out.

"I'll fall," I said, worriedly biting my lip.

"We'll never let you fall, Peppermint," Skarde said with a grin.

I loved how it looked on his face, and I couldn't help grinning back. My dark knight had finally let the past go, at least a little bit.

"That's right," Birger said, and Roar dipped his chin in agreement.

As a group, they pulled me out onto the ice. They showed me how to work the skates and not fall. They were patient instructors and caught me every time I stumbled. I wondered if the skating school needed more instructors because they'd be perfect. I smiled.

They were part of my world now. No longer under the grip of Loki's curse, they were free to be who they were. Birger gave a boisterous laugh, swinging me around until I was dizzy. Roar laid a hand on my arm or pushed my leg just so, his every action keeping an eye on me, and helping me along. Skarde sent little trails of magic through the air, and we oohed and aahed. Without the burden of the stone, his magic came back twice as strong and he was almost playful.

As they took me around the ice, I was so happy that I wasn't alone anymore. I had found my place, here in Silver Springs, with my friends and my mates. The guys and I had so much to learn from and about each other, and we were going to have a lifetime to do it. I couldn't ask for anything more. The loneliness I'd felt a short week ago seemed like a mirage.

Even my boss had agreed to give me more respect. When I'd stated my case, calmly and rationally, he'd agreed that he'd been too hard on me. He'd said how much he valued me as an employee. I couldn't believe it. He'd even accepted it when I said I was taking the rest of the week off and I'd be back on Monday.

But I wouldn't have even had the courage to approach him if Roar hadn't encouraged me. My Vikings were fierce, proud warriors, but they were also kind and generous. I grinned helplessly. I had my mates, and I knew I could take on the world.

# 21

# Pepper

Epilogue

I had never flown here before, but I'd never had a letter so important. The caves of the underworld were familiar to me. These halls were not. I could hear boisterous voices raised in song as I turned the corner into the great hall.

Men and women, warriors all, clustered around the tables enjoying a great feast. I dived through the sea of Vikings looking for her, for the one whose letter I carried. Their faces were curious as they looked up at me in cardinal form. I didn't think they got a lot of birds in Valhalla.

There she was, at the end of the row. Her blonde hair tied back in a braid, wearing a bright white polar bear fur, and laughing at something her neighbor had said. As soon as I landed, her blue eyes sought me out.

I studied her for a moment in bird form. Hel had done a good job at replicating her as an old woman, but she'd missed the boisterous cheer that made her truly Birger's daughter. I could see her father in her merry eyes. Shifting into human form, I leaned against the wooden table.

The Vikings around me drew back, some raising axes, hammers, or swords.

"Inge," I said, clearly and loudly. "I am a messenger from your father."

She stood and faced me, but she gestured for the others to put away their weapons. "I would hear his words, messenger," she said formally.

I took the letter out from my pocket, and I read out the words.

*Dearest Daughter, I am free from the curse at last. I returned to the world to find it much changed. Everything and everyone that I ever knew is gone, except for those who were cursed with me—Skarde and Roar. But we work to make a new life here, with our love and mate, Peppermint, by whose hand you receive this letter.*

*I miss you terribly and wish that I could have seen you grow and could have been there for every victorious moment. I am sorry, dearest Inge, that I could not be there now to see your great triumph and happy afterlife in Valhalla. I'm sorry for all that I missed, and I love you.*

*Signed, Birger.*

Inge gazed at me, tears glittering in her eyes, but in true warrior fashion, she did not let them fall. "He is happy?"

"Yes, I think so."

"You are his mate, beast-woman?"

I nodded.

"You must take good care of him," she said.

"I will."

"Good," she said with a smile. "I always wanted him to be happy."

I tilted my head. "You didn't blame him for going away?"

She shook her head. "I missed him, but he was a good man

and a good friend. He did what he thought was right."

"He'll be glad to hear that," I said, smiling. "I'm sorry I couldn't bring him here to see you. That was his greatest wish."

"I know," she said, bowing her head.

"You can't," a voice boomed behind me, "but he can."

I turned to see Thor dragging Loki down the aisle. The God of Thunder dropped his brother at Inge's feet.

"Bring her father here," Thor said.

"I don't owe these Vikings anything," Loki said. "You do it."

Thor put his hands on his hips and glowered at his brother. "You left them in the underworld for one thousand years."

"They stole from me," Loki said, standing and dusting himself off.

"You forgot about them," Thor said. "You wouldn't have even remembered if Hel hadn't said something."

Guilt flashed across Loki's face.

"You forgot about my father?" Her voice rising, Inge reached for her weapon.

I grabbed her and shook my head. "Wait."

"You have your stone. Give this woman back her father," Thor said, nodding to Inge.

Loki grimaced, but he waved his hand and Birger stood in front of us. He looked around, confusion on his face until he saw his daughter. Then his face lit up.

"Inge!" Birger cried, opening his arms.

She hugged him, and he lifted her off the ground like she was a child and not a grown woman. Happy tears streaked down both their faces.

I glanced over at Loki. "Thank you," I said.

He met my gaze for a brief minute, and I saw a hint of something there. I almost thought he'd wanted this all along.

He had bumped into me at the rink and helped us on the airplane—well, in typical Loki fashion.

Turning away, he said, "An hour, no more, then he returns to your world."

"Got it," I said.

Thor clapped a hand on Loki's shoulder as they walked away. "That wasn't so bad, was it?" Thor asked.

I chuckled and looked back at my Viking, finally getting to see his daughter again after all this time. He was the happiest I'd ever seen him. I could feel the pure joy of the moment humming down the mate bond. This was even better than a letter.

# UP NEXT

Fourteen more Silver Springs women get their own harems:

I moved to Silver Springs to escape my past, but then disaster strikes. I'm rejected by my fated mates and framed for a crime I didn't commit. I'm Zoe Wynter, the best magical maid in town, but my life is one mess no spells in the world can fix.

Can I have it all: the world title, the three gorgeous half angels who own the Silver Steins brewery and the chance to finally give Addie Ravenwood the middle finger? I'm Ember and I'm a hot mess on the ice but hopefully this time the rink won't melt!

When I'm dropped off in a little podunk town called Silver Springs under orders from my jerk of a father to turn their human newspaper from a money pit into a profitable business I want to scream. After meeting the sexy journalist that works there, a demon stripper, a reindeer shifter, and a selkie, they'll have me screaming for a whole different reason. I'm Neve and I'm the city girl who hated Silver Springs until my mates thawed my icy heart.

House sitting for Willow was supposed to be easy and fun. Instead, someone's playing tricks on me and I keep ending up naked in strange places with hot guys. And not just normal men, but a brooding god of the underworld, an 18th century Highlander and a swoon-worthy dragon shifter - although maybe that's not so bad. I'm Kari, and with all these sexy men around me, I'm sure to get my happily every after - aren't I?

My mates shift into dicks, throw their cocks around, lie to grow their penises... and raise hamburgers from the dead. I'm Storm, and my life has turned into chaos just when I need to save Silver Springs. It's a good thing I'm a raptor shifter, because detachable dicks and zombie cows ain't gonna cut it.

Freedom and dick, that's all I really want in life. First, I need to escape my ice-dicked fiancé and get to Silver Springs, a land of magical dildos where paranormal creatures run free. Then I need to find some sexy men to defile me in the dirtiest ways possible. Pound town, here comes Eirwen.

What do coffee, a manwhore incubus, a tender red fox, and a reclusive foxy artist have in common? Oh right. Me. Watch out for crazy pranks involving chickens, pussy glitter and blue dicks. But don't be fooled. Triple E will reign supreme and we will crush Cider. I'm Eirlys, get your caffeine ready and buckle up for the insane ride I'm gonna take you on.

The prank wars have ended. Of course, I was the winner. Regardless of what that vampire thinks. Hot Ciders' Snack Bar is the place to be. Until *they* start to move in, putting every store at the rink in risk. Not to mention it turns out I've acquired three mates, including Eirlys daddy vamp. I'm Cider and this is the story of my survival.

I moved to Silver Springs to enjoy a quiet life away from my family who wished for me to take a mate of their choosing. Sadly, there's no running from my family, and they send two potential suitors out to fetch me. Throw in the broody ice-phoenix who has fallen for me, and things are about to get heated. I'm Frostine, and things are about to get hot.

I'm just a cardinal shifter, and they are three fierce warriors. But when they're trapped in the underworld by Loki's curse, I'll do anything I can to save them, even armed only with a pair of ice skates and a letter. I'm Peppermint, and I'm a mail carrier, a klutzy bird shifter, and reluctant messenger to the dead.

What do a firefighter, a Fire Fae, and a husky shifter have in common? They all want a bite of Candela's cupcake.

I was happy dating emotionally unavailable men, especially after being rejected by my merc for hire mate, but now I'm reconsidering that after a night of body shots with my bestie's off-limits conjurer brother and hearing the passionate singing voice of the sexy funeral director. Should I break the rules so I can find my happiness or should I keep running from my past? I'm Misty, aka Gray, Silver Spring's second favorite tattoo artist.

Blacklisted in all of Hollywood, I need a job and a place to stay. Maybe my luck is about to change as I get hired as a photographer for the Silver Springs On Ice beauty pageant.

I have to re-learn how to ice skate but it's like riding a bike, right? I'm staying in a haunted B&B and I have the hots for my new boss and his annoying bodyguard. I'm Iclyn and I'm royally screwed.

I don't believe in witches, spells, fated mates—and I sure as hell don't believe in ice skating! I hate anything to do with cold weather and snow. *Nothing* is making *me* visit Silver Springs. . . I'm Aurora and this is my shitcicle of story.

New to town, running my own business, single mom...life can be super hard. Add in magical powers that, even in a town as accommodating as Silver Springs, I need to keep on the down low, and a daughter who's emerging powers are causing havoc, and I've got my hands full. Love? No thank you. Love x3? Hell no! I'm Lumi and this is my story of how fate has other ideas for me.

*Click here to discover all the books set in Silver Springs.*

Join our Silver Springs VIP community to stay up to date with all new releases and access exclusive stories, bonus scenes, giveaways, and more.

Want to receive news about Silver Springs?  Subscribe to the Silver Springs Herald!

Turn the page for a preview of Candela, the next book in the Silver Skates series.

# Candela

Another day in Silver Springs.

Another day without answers.

Sighing, I back into the swinging kitchen door, pivoting through it and into the front of my quaint cupcake shop. I like my shop. The glitter sparkling like fresh snow on frosting makes me smile, and I pause behind the glass container full of cupcakes. My eyes drift along the varying colors and flavors before I slide the new batch of my specialty salted caramel cupcakes into the empty space on the top shelf.

*There.*

A couple walks by the window, pausing to read my sign and peer into the window at the colorful shelves full of sweets. My polite smile fades as they turn and continue walking down the sidewalk.

*Today is just not my day.*

Jasper huffs and he rubs his wet snout against my hand, making me giggle.

"I know, boy. It's just the rumor mill ruining business again. It'll blow over, right?"

Jasper barks his agreement. The string of strange fires around Silver Springs are rumored to be a curse, one caused by me.

"Remind me to change my name," I complained. It didn't slip past my notice that this town was filled with girls with themed names. Those with jewel-type names seem to all be happy, as well as those with flower names.

I had noticed a trend recently as well. Winter or Christmas-themed names seem to be the new promise for prosperity and happiness. I'm superstitious when it suits me.

Right now? I could use some damn luck.

Another couple walks by my shop, pointedly avoiding looking into the window.

"I'm the one who's cursed," I say, holding back the ache in my voice. "Candela is a Christmas name, right? I was born on Christmas. But what if the latest spell is about the season and not the holiday? Would having a name that associates with fire put me on the negative end of the scale?"

Jasper whines, telling me that I'm definitely overthinking this.

It never ceases to amaze me how well my faithful husky seems to pick up on my emotions. Sometimes he knows I'm upset before I ever realize it myself.

I scratch his favorite spot behind his ears before sinking into the pink fuzzy lounge behind the tall glass counter. If I slouch far enough, I can only see the shelves of my store's cupcakes on display, leaving my view of the rest of the town blocked out entirely.

"It just feels like I don't belong here sometimes," I told Jasper, cupping his fluffy face in both of my hands as he sat in-between my legs. He seems to listen attentively, although he's heard my sobfest about a thousand times.

It's a good thing that he can't repeat anything I've said, or the gossip mill would be a churnin' through town. Jasper would be a total tattletale.

"I don't have any magic of my own," I complain. "I'm just a plain 'ol boring human. What was I thinking setting up a cupcake shop in a place Silver Springs?"

It's obvious to me by now that humans are *not* supposed to see all the supernatural shenanigans that go on in this town. And yet, I do, which means something is definitely wrong with me.

Jasper whines again. His too-intelligent blue eyes stare at me, full of mischief and wisdom just like always and the answer seems to pop right into my head.

You're here b*ecause you need answers, and if we're going to find them, it'll be in a place like this.*

Right, a place full of witches, vampires, and ice block shifters. Piece of cake.

Or, *cupcake*, as it were.

I pat the couch, urging Jasper to jump up beside me. Then I slouch a little further and lean my head onto his fluffy coat. His surplus of fur makes him a good pillow, until that one stray hair makes you sneeze, anyway. Besides that, he's a great listener. I've been talking to him so much that my brain has been supplying suitable responses, which probably means I've officially gone insane.

Because I'm still talking to a dog.

*Husky,* that little voice corrects in my mind, sounding exasperated.

Yep. I've gone insane.

"Same difference," I complain out loud as I close my eyes and try to imagine I'm anywhere else.

It's not that I don't like Silver Springs. It's more that I'm frustrated, and I'm tired of pretending to be someone I'm not. The exhaustion of it is finally wearing me down.

I could let the residents know I can see everything... that I know everything.

Jasper barks as a red fox bounds toward the window. She stops and sniffs at the glass, as if considering coming in.

"That's just Cider in her fox form," I remind him, tugging at his fur to keep him in place. Jasper doesn't leave my side very often, but if he sees anything else furry, he tends to have dog-brain. "Don't chase her again or I'm going to tell her to stop giving you treats!"

He wines and lowers his snout. The little fox peers inside, and it breaks my heart to pretend not to notice.

I could do it right now. I could look at her and wave, or say something, or just invite her inside, right?

She seems to notice my hesitation and paws at the glass, and for a minute I wonder if she's going to shift right there. It wouldn't be the first time a shifter had a cupcake craving and bolted straight to my door in the fasted form they could manage on four legs.

Except, something inside of me just isn't ready. I can't do it. I hold my breath until she leaves.

*You need to open up one of these days,* that voice tells me.

I know he's right. Yet, I can't find myself capable of opening up or trusting anyone. Not even Cider, who's always nice to me. She always gives Jasper treats, too, which makes me like her even more. Despite my threats, I'd never take Cider's sweet gesture away.

To my surprise, the front bell dings and a completely naked Cider walks in, her smile beaming as she waves.

"Hey, Candela! Oh! I thought I smelled a new batch of cupcakes."

Grab your copy of Candela here.

# ABOUT THE AUTHOR

**Cali Mann** is the author of the Thornbriar Academy series and Misfit of Thornbriar Academy series as well as many others. She writes paranormal romance, the sexy kind with why choose, hunky shifters, sexy vampires, and women who stand up for themselves. She learned romance by reading through her mother's entire Gothic romance collection in her teens so she and dark romance go way back. When she's not writing, she spends her time streaming shows, playing video games, and pestering her two tuxedo cats.

*Say hello to Cali online:*
www.calimann.com

www.facebook.com/groups/calispack
www.facebook.com/calimannauthor/

# ALSO BY CALI MANN

**Thornbriar Academy series**
Found
Bound
Saved

**Misfit of Thornbriar Academy**
Infiltrate
Destroy

**Hell-Baited Wolves**
Called
Scorned
Unleashed

Printed in Great Britain
by Amazon

14523935R00099